Face-to-face, with only the pulpit between them, they stood smiling at each other as if they had just uncovered a buried treasure.

Josephine, exactly at that moment, noticed Logan's eyes. Yes, she had seen his eyes before. But she hadn't really noticed how incredibly beautiful they were—such a dark, rich brown that they reminded her of expensive black satin.

"What?" he asked her, in a half curious, half-amused manner.

His single-word question snapped her out of it—she had been unintentionally staring into his eyes. Once she realized that she had been mindlessly ogling him, she started to laugh.

"Sorry—I was just thinking about something from when I was a kid."

"What's that?"

"When I was...oh, I don't know...seven or eight..." Josephine walked out from behind the pulpit and joined Logan where he was standing.

"I used to stand in this exact spot and pretend that I was getting married. Jordan and I took turns officiating the wedding and being the bride..." Josephine laughed softly and looked over at him. "You standing here just reminded me of that. I haven't thought of that in years."

THE BRANDS OF MONTANA:
Wrangling their own happily-ever-afters

Dear Reader,

Thank you for selecting *A Match Made in Montana*, the first book in The Brands of Montana miniseries! *A Match Made in Montana* is the romantic friends-to-lovers story of Logan Wolf and Josephine Brand. I always knew that laid-back Logan Wolf, the hot motorcycle cop who had a cameo at the beginning of *The One He's Been Looking For*, would be the perfect match for Jordan's (*A Baby for Christmas*, *The One He's Been Looking For*, *Marry Me, Mackenzie!*) twin sister, Josephine. In Logan's arms, Josephine learns how to let go of the past and embrace the future. In Josephine's arms, Logan learns how to trust himself enough to love again. And it all unfolds in the beautiful mountains of Montana.

Ever since my parents took me on a family vacation to a Montana working ranch when I was twelve years old, I have been hooked on Big Sky Country. So to have a Harlequin Special Edition miniseries set in Montana is particularly sweet for me. Many of the places that you will experience in *A Match Made in Montana* were pulled directly from my childhood memories. But as much as I love my old memories of Montana, I love creating new memories with the Brand family at Bent Tree Ranch even more. Be sure to look out for more The Brands of Montana romances, and I invite you to stop by joannasimsromance.com for a visit!

Happy reading!

Joanna

PS: Special thanks to MM for the inspiration!

A Match
Made in Montana

—

Joanna Sims

HARLEQUIN® SPECIAL EDITION®

Recycling programs
for this product may
not exist in your area.

ISBN-13: 978-0-373-65886-2

A Match Made in Montana

Copyright © 2015 by Joanna Sims

Printed in U.S.A.

Joanna Sims lives in Florida with her awesome husband, Cory, and their three fabulous felines, Sebastian, Chester (aka Tubby) and Ranger. By day, Joanna works as a speech-language pathologist, and by night, she writes contemporary romance for Harlequin Special Edition. Joanna loves to hear from Harlequin readers and invites you to stop by her website for a visit: joannasimsromance.com.

Books by Joanna Sims

Harlequin Special Edition

Marry Me, Mackenzie!
The One He's Been Looking For
A Baby for Christmas

Visit the Author Profile page at Harlequin.com for more titles.

This book is dedicated, with love, to my Dad.
In the whole entire world, you are the best dad for me!

Chapter One

"Man…" Lieutenant Wolf checked his watch. "I can't believe I got stuck working overtime the day I'm supposed to start my leave."

"Don't worry about it…I've got this. Why don't you take off?" Officer Cook asked.

"I appreciate it, but I don't feel right cutting out early. I'll just give my friends a call and let them know that…" Logan stopped midsentence, his attention was drawn to a silver car speeding their way. "Wait a minute…wait a minute…how fast are *they* going?"

Logan stepped closer to the side of the road, aimed his radar gun at the car, and clocked it breaking the speed limit by twenty-one miles per hour. Logan acted on pure instinct, sprang into action. He jumped onto the road, jerked his arm to the left, finger pointed at the side of the road.

"Pull over! *Now!*" Logan yelled at the driver. He stood his ground with his feet planted on the black asphalt until he saw the driver slow down and turn on their signal.

"That's reckless, right there…" Cook came up beside him.

"Sure is." Logan nodded.

Logan handed the radar gun off to his partner, grabbed his clipboard and pen, and then headed across the two lanes separating him from the car he had just flagged down. Giving this driver a well-deserved ticket was the last thing he was going to do before he went on leave.

Josephine Brand glanced over her shoulder to see the motorcycle cop striding across the lanes in her direction. She went back to frantically riffling through her glove box to find her most current insurance and registration information. She *always* kept everything together neatly in a labeled envelope in the glove box on top of the car manual. But…it wasn't *there*!

"I can't believe this is *happening*…" Josephine shut the glove box and went back to searching in her wallet.

She was already late, and she *hated* to be late so she made it a point never to *be* late. But she had gotten into an argument with her boyfriend, Brice, the night before and their disagreement had followed them into the next morning. They rarely fought, but when they did fight, it was usually a knock-down, drag-out affair. She was exhausted from lack of sleep, emotionally drained from fighting, and now she was going to get her first speeding ticket in years.

"Great…" she muttered. "Just *great*."

When the second search through her wallet was unfruitful, Josephine let out a quick, frustrated sigh and shoved the wallet back into her purse. License out and ready to be handed over, Josephine rested her head in her hand and waited for her inevitable ticket.

"Afternoon, miss." Logan had already surveyed the car and the driver as he crossed the street. Nothing looked suspicious, so he intended to treat this like a routine traffic stop.

"Good afternoon, Officer," she said respectfully and extended her license to him.

Logan positioned himself by the side-view mirror, his body facing oncoming traffic, his feet out of the line of the tires. He accepted her license, clipped it to the clipboard.

"Do you know how fast you were going?"

"No." Josephine slipped her sunglasses to the top of her head so he could see her eyes. "I'm sorry...I don't."

She had been stressed out about being late to the airport, and her mind had still been distracted by the fight with Brice, so she just hadn't been paying attention.

From the beginning, Logan had noticed that the driver was an attractive woman, much in the same way he had noticed the model of car she was driving. It was his job to notice everything about his stops. And taking inventory of drivers and passengers was routine. So, yes, he noticed that her hair was long and golden-brown, that the hair framed her oval face, and that her frowning lips were naturally pink. But when she lifted her sunglasses and looked up at him, he was temporarily captivated by her stunning aqua-blue eyes.

Annoyed that he had allowed himself to be distracted from his purpose, Logan shifted his weight and refocused his mind on the task at hand. He had a job to do and he needed to get it done.

"The posted speed limit here is thirty-five. I clocked you at fifty-six miles per hour," Logan said. "Twenty miles over the posted speed limit is considered reckless driving."

Josephine's eyes widened, her lips parted slightly. "*Reckless driving?* No. That can't be right. I swear to you, Officer, I wasn't speeding intentionally," Josephine explained quickly. "I haven't had a ticket in *ten years*. When you look me up, you'll see. I have a perfect driving record..."

She could tell by the lack of expression on the officer's face that he wasn't remotely swayed by her explanation. He waited quietly for her to finish, then he asked for her proof of insurance and registration.

"I don't have them..." Josephine admitted. "I always keep them right there in my glove box..." She gestured to her glove box. "I just received my new registration. I think I must have just forgotten to put the envelope back in the car. But, I promise you, I have a current registration and valid insurance."

The officer gave one slight nod of his head, wrote something down on his clipboard, then walked to the front of her car to write down her tag number.

"I'll be back," he said to her before he headed back to his motorcycle parked in the median.

Josephine hit the steering wheel with the palms of her hands and dropped her head back. Now she was *really* late, and if this cop wanted to be a real jerk, he could easily cite her with reckless driving! Why couldn't she flirt her way out of stuff like some of her friends did? She'd never been good at flirting or using her femininity to get her way. She always felt stupid when she tried to flirt and it usually backfired anyway. So she didn't bother to try anymore.

While she waited for the cop to return, she called her twin sister, Jordan.

"I'm running a little late, Jordy." She didn't offer a reason why and she was glad when Jordan didn't ask.

"Don't worry about it. The plane can't leave without you." Unlike her, Jordan had never been uptight about sticking to a schedule.

Josephine noticed the cop heading her way and tried to rush off the phone. "I've got to go, okay? But, I should be there in fifteen or twenty minutes."

"It's all good," Jordan said before they hung up the phone. For once, her sister's cavalier attitude about being on time came in handy.

"I'm going to have to give you three citations today, Ms. Brand. One for lack of proof of insurance, one for failing to produce your vehicle registration, and one for speeding." Logan handed her the clipboard and a pen. "I'll need to get your signature on the bottom of all three citations."

Josephine felt the blood drain from her face; her heart beat faster. She'd *never* gotten that many tickets at one time! She had a spotless driving record, and yet this cop couldn't show her even one little ounce of mercy? All of her internal frustration flowed into her tense fingers; she gripped the pen so tightly that her knuckles turned white. The lines of her signatures were heavy, dark and smudgy.

When she was finished, she slapped the pen onto the top of the first citation, handed the clipboard back to the officer and then slid her sunglasses back down over her eyes. Since she couldn't, at the moment, look at the of-

ficer with the respect she felt his uniform deserved, she
didn't want him to be able to see her eyes at all.

Logan quickly finished the transaction, separated her
copy of the citations from his, handed them to her with
her driver's license.

"You'll note that I didn't cite you with reckless driving," the officer said. "And, once you show proof of insurance and current vehicle registration, the other two
citations will be dropped."

Well, that was something at least; he'd dropped the
reckless driving charge. Josephine folded the tickets
neatly in half and tucked them into her purse. It sounded,
to her ears, that the officer sounded almost...*sorry*...that
he'd had to give her that many tickets. But it certainly
hadn't stopped him from throwing the book at her!

When she turned her face back to the officer, she
noticed that he had taken his sunglasses off. She was
immediately drawn, naturally drawn, to his eyes. They
were such a dark, rich brown that they were very nearly
as black as his pupils. His gaze was direct, and there was
a moment, a flash second, when she thought that she had
caught a glimpse of this man's soul.

"On a personal note, are you related to Jordan Brand?"
the officer surprised her by asking.

"She's my sister." Josephine replied stiffly. "You know
her?"

"I actually pulled her over downtown about a year
ago," Logan explained.

"I'm not surprised." Josephine retorted. "Unlike me,
Jordy speeds all the time."

"Well..." Logan hadn't missed the sarcasm. "All I can
say is that I'm sorry that we met under these circumstances and it's actually ironic because..."

"Look..." Josephine cut him off. Was this guy *really* going to try to pick her up when he'd just written her *three* tickets? "Am I free to go? I'm really late..."

"Yes. You're free to go." The officer put his sunglasses back on and stepped away from her car. "Drive safely, Ms. Brand."

Josephine ran through the private airport, lugging two overstuffed carry-on bags on each shoulder, and dragging one oversize rolling suitcase behind her. She had never been to Montgomery Airport in San Diego before, but she had printed out a map of the facility the night before and highlighted the quickest route to her destination. She had been raised on a Montana ranch, but she had learned how to run in high heels years ago. Up on the ball of the foot and full steam ahead!

"I'm so sorry I'm late!" Josephine called out to her sister, Jordan. Jordan was standing in front of her fiancé's private jet, occupied with her phone.

Jordan looked up, spotted her, and smiled brightly. Her sister jogged over to greet her with a warm hug.

"Relax, sis!" Jordan said. "You know that nothing's set in stone for me."

Jordan slipped one of the bags off her shoulder, and the bag dropped to the ground with a dull thud. "Uh... *wow*, Jo. What in the heck did you pack?"

"Textbooks." She would be a third-year law student in the fall and the suggested summer reading list had been *pages* long. "I hope I brought enough."

"Trust me, you brought enough," Jordan said teasingly. "I just hope your bags don't put us over our weight restriction. We might have to make a tough choice between you and your books."

"Haha, very funny." Jordan had always picked on her about her overachieving ways. They were more than twins, more than sisters; they were best friends. But they were complete opposites. Jordan was a professional artist, a painter, who had dropped out of graduate school to pursue her passion. Josephine, on the other hand, could never stop something before she finished it. She finished everything she started, and she finished it *well*.

Together, they walked the short distance to Ian's jet.

"I can't believe that this is the start of your wedding trip, Jordy." Both sisters stopped walking and talking at the same time; they looked at each other, and easily read each other's thoughts.

"Holy crap, Jo! I'm getting *married*!" Jordan shook her head in disbelief.

"You're getting married." Josephine smiled, her eyes starting to tear from a mixture of happiness for her sister and sadness for the changes that would inevitably follow. Nothing ever stayed the same.

"OMG, don't start crying already!" Jordan hugged her again. "I swear, between Mom and you, there's not gonna be one tissue left in the entire state of Montana."

Josephine laughed and brushed the tears out of her eyelashes. "I'll do my best to keep the waterworks to a minimum…at least until the ceremony. After that, no deal."

"Well, of course you have to cry at the ceremony," her twin said as Josephine rolled her large suitcase over to the cargo area for the pilot to load.

"Hey, you got my message that Brice won't be joining us, right?" Josephine asked.

"Yeah, what's up with that?" Jordan put her hands

on her slender hips. "Is everything okay with the two of you?"

"Well, actually, that's why I was…" Josephine started to say.

Jordan got distracted by a man walking through the airplane hangar.

"Captain Stern!" her sister yelled and waved her hand in the air. To her, she said, "Hold that thought, Jo. That's our pilot and I need to tell him something before I forget."

"Okay." Maybe she shouldn't tell her sister about the fight with Brice anyway. Her family, especially Jordan, had never really been fond of him.

Jordan started the walk over to the waiting pilot; she turned around and walked backward for a few steps.

"Why don't you go get settled?" her sister suggested. "Ian'll tell you where to find the booze. He only stocks the best."

Josephine lugged the carry-on bag loaded with textbooks up the small flight of stairs that led up to the main cabin of the jet. She'd seen pictures of the jet, of course, but to see it in person was an entirely different experience. The cabin was decked out in sophisticated grays and blacks and accented with polished mahogany. There was a long leather couch on one side, while the other had two separate seating areas with oversize recliners and a small table in between. In the back, there was a narrow hallway that led back to a bedroom and en-suite bathroom.

Ian Sterling, Jordan's fiancé, was sitting on the couch. Next to Ian's left leg sat a muscular black Labrador retriever.

"It's me, Ian," Josephine said to her soon-to-be brother-in-law.

"I thought I heard your voice." Ian stood up to greet her. He was a model-handsome man and world-famous for his photography. But a rare eye disease had recently destroyed his central vision, rendering him legally blind and sidetracking his career as a professional photographer.

Josephine hugged Ian; it made her feel really good that Jordan had found her perfect match in Ian Sterling. She had never seen two people as crazy for each other as they were.

"And who's your friend?" Jordan had finally managed, after nearly a year of trying, to convince Ian to get a service dog.

"Shadow." Ian rested his hand proudly on the dog's head.

"Is it okay if I pet him?"

"At ease, Shadow," Ian commanded gently.

Shadow's body language changed on the command and he started to wag his tail.

"Shake, Shadow." Ian gave the Lab a second command.

Shadow immediately extended his right paw to her. Josephine took the paw, smiled, and gave it a shake.

"It's very nice to meet you, Shadow."

Josephine had already set up her computer and unloaded her books in the short time it took for her sister to appear. Jordan plopped down next to her fiancé, tucked her long legs to the side of her body, and frowned at her.

"I hope it's not going to be like this our entire trip, Jo," Jordan complained.

"I'm not going to spend all of my time studying, but I

can't just pretend like I'm not in school for two months. The third year is a make-it-or-break-it year. That's when they really try to thin out the herd."

"You always say that about everything and then you always end up on top." Jordan rolled her eyes.

"Quit bugging her about it." Ian put his arm around Jordan's shoulder and pulled her tightly to his side. "Not everyone waits to the last minute to get things done like you do, beautiful."

Josephine smiled triumphantly at Jordan. She finished arranging her collection of items in an orderly and precise way: a book stand held a thick constitutional law book upright, her laptop and tablet were both charging, three differently colored highlighter pens were situated in a perfectly even row.

"There…" She surveyed her work. "This is perfect."

"I need a drink." Jordan stood up. "Anyone care to join me?"

"I'm good." Josephine sat down in the large recliner and used the controls to adjust it perfectly to her body. "Shouldn't we be getting ready to take off soon?"

"We'll leave as soon as our fourth arrives," Ian told her.

Josephine glanced at her sister. "Didn't Jordy tell you that Brice couldn't make it?"

"I told him." Jordan poured herself a scotch on the rocks.

"Then who are we waiting for?" she asked.

"My best man is catching a ride with us," Ian explained.

Josephine turned the swiveling recliner toward the couch. "Wait a minute. Dylan is coming with us? I can't believe he agreed to come without Mackenzie and Hope."

"Oh! That's right! You don't know…" Jordan returned to her spot next to Ian.

"Know what?"

"Mackenzie has been having some issues with her pregnancy and her doctors don't want her to fly."

"I didn't know that," Josephine said, concerned.

Ian's best friend, Dylan Axel, was married to their cousin, Mackenzie, and they were expecting their second child together.

"So, Dylan had to beg off being Ian's best man."

"I'm so sorry to hear that. I had no idea that Mackenzie was having a rough pregnancy."

Sometimes law school was like living in a bubble. There were a lot of times that she just didn't have contact with the world outside of school. She would turn off her phone, ignore all forms of social media, and she would focus all of her energy on studying.

"I'll have to call her," Josephine said aloud to herself before she asked, "Who's going to stand in for Dylan?"

"One of my old friends from high school," Ian said.

Jordan smiled brightly. "You're gonna love him, Jo! He's such a cool guy. And what's really funny is that he was actually there the day that Ian and I first met…"

"I think I hear him now." Ian nodded toward the direction of the door.

Josephine heard two animated male voices coming from just outside of the jet. Then, she heard the sound of heavy, decisive footsteps heading up the metal stairs to the jet's cabin.

Josephine looked at the doorway curiously; both Ian and Jordan stood up.

"It's real nice of you to finally show up, Logan!" Jordan called out to the best man teasingly.

Logan Wolf, still in his uniform, stepped into the jet's cabin.

"Hey…" Logan smiled charmingly at Jordan. "Don't blame me, blame the San Diego PD."

Jordan hugged Logan in greeting before he shook hands with Ian.

"I'm glad you could make it, man," Ian said.

"I appreciate the invitation," Logan replied. He could feel Josephine's eyes on him, but he'd deliberately waited to look her way.

"Logan, I'd like you to meet my sister, Josephine."

Josephine stood up and extended her hand.

"Oh…" Her eyes locked onto Logan's. "Trust me… we've already met."

Chapter Two

"Wait, *what*?" Jordan asked, her expression a mixture of surprise and intrigue.

"Officer…Wolf, is it?" Josephine slipped her fingers free of his.

Logan rested the duffel bag on the seat next to him and smiled warmly at her. "Lieutenant, actually, but I think it's all right for you to call me Logan now, Josephine."

"Hell-*o*?" Her sister was impatient for details.

"As it turns out…" Josephine paused, looked skyward with a little shake of her head, before she continued. "Logan is the reason why I was late."

Logan told Jordan and Ian, "I pulled her over for speeding."

And here it comes, Josephine thought.

Jordan's eyes lit up, as did her face. First, she smiled broadly like a Cheshire cat, and then she tipped her head back to laugh out loud.

"You got a *ticket*?" Jordan gleefully exclaimed. "Holy *crap*! Miss 'I haven't gotten a ticket in ten years' *actually* got a *ticket*?"

Logan said, "She shared that fact with me during the stop."

"Of course she did," her sister chirped. "Trying to worm her way out of the ticket, no doubt."

"Don't you think that you're just a little too happy about this, Jordy? I mean, really." Josephine had her arms crossed over her chest, not enjoying this conversation nearly as much as Jordan.

Ian had taken his seat and Jordan flopped down next to him. "Oh, please, you know exactly why I'm enjoying this so much!" To Logan, her sister said, "You have to understand, Jo has been harassing me about my driving for *years*!"

"In my defense," Josephine explained to Logan, "Jordy has had her license revoked *twice*."

"Irrelevant!" her sister exclaimed. "Because *now* you can't wear your perfect driving record like a badge of honor when you're lecturing me about *my* driving."

"You are a menace to drivers everywhere." Josephine had relaxed her arms as she relaxed into the conversation. "You ride that Ducati of yours like you're a bat out of hell."

"I'm a great driver." Jordan put her hand on Ian's leg to get his attention. "You trust me when I drive, don't you?"

"Absolutely not," Ian replied with a deadpan expression. "I am grateful every day that I can afford a driver."

"That's a horrible thing to say, GQ!" Jordan punched her fiancé lightly on the arm. "Now do you see what I have to put up with, Logan?"

"I do see," Logan nodded thoughtfully, playing along.

"That is why you are officially my hero for the day." Jordan pointed at Logan.

"But let's be clear," Josephine said. "He's not a hero for putting on a uniform every day and risking his life. You're saying he's a hero for giving me a ticket so I can't harass you about your terrible driving anymore. Right?"

"What's your point?" Jordan asked with a shrug.

Josephine looked at Logan. "Do you see what *I* have to put up with?"

"You're in a no-win situation, buddy," Ian warned his longtime friend.

"I see that, too," Logan laughed good-naturedly, then lifted the duffel bag off the seat. "Hey, before we take off, I'd like to change out of this monkey suit into some street clothes."

"Straight back to the bedroom." Ian pointed in the direction of the back of the jet. "You can change in there."

"If you'll excuse me, then. I came here straight from work and I'd really like to feel like I've started my vacation." Logan's arm brushed Josephine's when he walked past her to get to the back of the jet.

It wasn't long before Logan returned carrying the duffel bag in one hand and a garment bag in his other.

"Is there some place I can hang up my uniform?" he asked.

"Closet's right there." Jordan pointed. "You can put your bag in there, too, if you want. While you were in the back, the pilot said that we're about ready to taxi out to the runway, so grab a seat and make yourself comfortable."

Logan did just that. After he hung up his uniform and stowed his bag, he took the seat across from Josephine's recliner. Logan Wolf had been noticeably handsome in his uniform, and he was just as attractive in his crisp jeans, tucked-in short-sleeved green polo and San Diego Padres baseball cap. She was in a long-term relationship, yes, but she still had eyes and could see if a man was good-looking or not. Logan was a good-looking man. But then again, so was her Brice.

Thinking of Brice, Josephine checked her phone to see if he had called her. When she left for the airport, things were still *messy* between them. Normally, he would have called her by now; he would have tried to smooth things over before her flight. But this time, he hadn't. What did that mean?

Not wanting to spend the beginning of her sister's wedding trip dwelling on her problems with Brice, Josephine turned off her phone and prompted Jordan to tell her all about the latest wedding plans. Ever since she was a young girl, she had loved all things wedding, and hearing about all of the latest details of her twin's upcoming nuptials would be the exact distraction she needed.

While Jordan excitedly shared the latest details of her wedding with her, the pilot taxied the jet out to the runway and they took off for Helena, Montana, soon after. Jordan, who had always been a nervous flier, had stopped talking and held on tightly to Ian's arm while the jet quickly ascended to the level of the clouds. Once the jet leveled off, Jordan opened her eyes again.

"You're much better than you used to be, that's for sure," Josephine complimented her sister.

Jordan hugged her fiancé's arm more tightly and smiled at him. "Being with Ian has really helped me."

"Not as much as being with you has helped me." Ian brought her hand up to his lips and kissed it.

Josephine was so happy for her sister. But she felt a twinge of jealousy whenever she saw Jordan with Ian. He loved her so much; it was plain to see in the way he spoke to her, the way he spoke about her and in the way he touched her. She knew that Brice loved her, but he wasn't, by nature, a demonstrative person. And even though she had accepted that part of Brice's personality, she couldn't stop herself from *craving* what her sister had found.

Ian tried, unsuccessfully, to stifle a yawn. "I'm sorry, guys…I promise it's not the company."

"You do look tired, Ian." Josephine had noticed that earlier.

"He didn't sleep well last night," Jordan explained, holding his hand. "Why don't you go lie down, baby?"

"I'm not just going to leave all of you out here while I sleep." Ian shook his head.

But both Logan and Josephine assured him that it would be okay with them, and Ian appeared to be so tired that it didn't take much convincing. He kissed Jordan and stood up.

"Bedroom, Shadow." He gave the black Lab the command, which Shadow immediately followed.

When Ian disappeared into the bedroom, out of earshot, Jordan confided in them.

"Ian's been having a really hard time sleeping. The specialist says that it's not uncommon for people with Stargardt to have a sleep disorder. He's been on melatonin, but it's not really helping all the much. Honestly, we were both up all night last night."

"Then you need to go back and get some rest, too," Josephine told her.

"What about you guys?" Jordan rubbed her eyes tiredly.

"I've got plenty of reading to do," Josephine assured her.

Logan nodded his agreement and held up his earbuds. "And I'm going to kick back and listen to music. Don't worry about us. We'll be fine. Go get some rest."

Like Ian, Jordan didn't take much convincing. When they were alone together, Logan said jokingly, "And then there were two..."

Josephine smiled faintly; she hoped that he really was going to listen to music and didn't expect her to entertain him now that they were the only two left in the main cabin. She had so much summer reading to do that until she got started with it and finished it, it felt like a giant albatross around her neck.

"I really do have a lot of reading to do." She tried to remind him politely that she needed to concentrate.

"And I really am going to listen to music," he countered easily; he put his earbuds in his ears, fiddled with his phone, leaned back his head, and closed his eyes.

Josephine couldn't hear any sound coming from his earbuds over the noise of the jet. There wasn't one excuse left not to open the first textbook and get to work. She took in a deep breath, let it out and relaxed her shoulders at the same time, and then took the book off the stand and set it down on the table directly in front of her. The spine of the thick book was stiff as she cracked it open for the first time. Josephine took the cap off a fresh, yellow highlighter pen, grabbed a black ballpoint pen, and held them together in her right hand. When she studied, she had her own system of highlighting, underlining information, and tabbing pages. Armed with her study utensils, she began the daunting task of wading through the first few pages of her textbook.

After trudging valiantly through the first, tedious chapter, Josephine leaned back in her chair, closed her eyes, and tried to rub the soreness out of her neck. She wished she could just throw all of her textbooks out the window so she could enjoy her first trip home in years, but there was just too much to do. There was still way too much information that she didn't know or understand. And unfortunately, at the moment, her brain was repelling all new information. Josephine breathed in deeply through her nose and then let it out on a long, tired sigh. She gathered up her cache of studying devices and neatly put them back into their proper places. The one thing that had led to her success above all else was her determination to stay organized. That was her lifeline to sanity, as well as success.

Lounging across from her, Logan had been impatiently waiting for Josephine to stop studying. He didn't really want to listen to music alone at the very beginning of his first real vacation in years. He wanted to celebrate, but he also respected that Josephine was dedicated to her studies. Periodically, he would open his eyes to see if she was done reading. He checked five times throughout the hour, but it wasn't until the sixth time that he caught Josephine rubbing her eyes. The minute he saw Josephine start to pack up her books and computer, Logan switched off his music and pulled the earbuds out of his ears.

"Taking a break?" he asked hopefully.

Josephine nodded, yawned, and carefully wound the cord of her computer neatly and secured it properly with the provided Velcro.

"I'm trying to get ready for my last year, but I'm afraid that my brain has hit its saturation level." Josephine slipped the computer into its designated spot and then zipped the bag shut.

Logan stood up and stretched. "I was thinking about raiding the liquor cabinet. Care to join me?"

"You know what? I think I would." Josephine's first thought was "no," but her verbal answer switched to a "yes." "You'll find the liquor right across from the closet."

"Jackpot!" Logan opened the cabinet with a smile. "What's your poison?"

"You don't happen to see any gin in there, do you?"

Logan pulled out a black bottle and held it up for her to see. "Hendricks okay?"

Josephine gave a slight nod, a small smile. "Have you ever made a martini?"

"Before I was a cop? Bartender..." Logan found two martini glasses, vermouth, and olives.

"Um, I usually like just a hint of vermouth and two olives." Josephine leaned forward a bit. "Please."

"Why don't you let me make you a martini my way? I don't want to brag, but I was pretty well-known for my martini."

Josephine wasn't really adventurous with her food or her drinks. She knew what she liked, she liked what she liked, and she stuck to what she liked. If she didn't like Logan's martini, she wouldn't be able to grin and bear it quietly.

"Okay, give this a try. I hope you don't mind your martinis dirty." Logan carefully handed her the martini glass and then sat down across from her.

"To Ian and Jordan." Logan held his glass out to her.

"Jordan and Ian." Josephine touched her glass to his with a tired smile.

Josephine knew Logan was watching her as she took a small sip of the martini. She never drank her martinis dirty and she typically preferred the taste of Tanqueray. Logan's martini was different, the tangy taste unusual, but it was surprisingly…

"Mmm." Josephine's eyes widened with pleasure. "This is really good…"

"I have a 100 percent satisfaction-guaranteed record with my martini…" Logan slid the two olives off the toothpick into his mouth.

"But, you don't want to brag," Josephine teased him before she took a slightly bigger sip. "I have to be honest. I wasn't expecting to like it. Normally, I only like the way my boyfriend makes a martini."

Logan stopped chewing the olives for a second when he heard the word "boyfriend." Up until now, Josephine hadn't mentioned a significant other, so Logan was starting to believe that he might have a shot of taking her out on a date while they were in Montana together. From the moment he looked into Josephine's eyes, he'd wanted to ask her out. He was really attracted to Jordan's beautiful sister, more so than he had been to any woman for a really long time, and it was just his rotten luck that she was taken. Of course, she was taken…why wouldn't she be?

Disappointed, Logan raised his glass up in the air a little. "I respect any man who can make a decent martini."

Josephine laughed. "I think Brice was probably weaned on martinis."

"Is that right?" he asked out of politeness, but he really didn't want to hear about the guy who was currently seeing the woman he wanted to date.

"I'm going to have another." Logan finished his drink, stood up. "Are you still good with that one?"

Josephine nodded and showed him that she still had some left in her glass. She wasn't much of a drinker and the last thing she wanted to do was arrive home for the first time in years tipsy.

"Come to think of it," she added, half thinking aloud, "I never drank martinis until I met Brice. We met in college and then we ended up deciding to go to law school together. He's a couple of years ahead of me, so he's already graduated, passed the California Bar, and taken a job with a firm in Van Nuys." She paused to take another small sip of her drink. "He practices environmental law, which is why he can't come join me in Montana until right before the wedding... He was just given a really big case."

Wanting to bring the conversation back to his point of interest, which was *her*, he asked, "What kind of law do you want to practice?"

"Oh!" Josephine's face lit up. "Well, my dream ever since I was in high school has been to work for the Southern Poverty Law Center. Have you ever heard of them?"

Logan shook his head "no."

"They've been fighting for the civil rights of marginalized and poor communities for years. And I know I would love to do that work."

"But?" He heard a definite *but* at the end of her sentence.

Josephine sighed and shrugged, thought for a second or two before she answered him. "But I don't think that it's practical to think that I'll work for them one day."

"Why not?"

"Because, for one thing, they need experienced litigators for the types of cases that they handle, so I'd have to get that experience first."

"That shouldn't be a problem for someone like you, and we have plenty of people in our state who need defending." He smiled at her. "I arrest 'em, you defend 'em."

That made her laugh, before she said, "But they really only operate out of the South, so…"

"That's what moving vans are for."

Josephine finished off her drink, and placed the empty glass carefully on the table. "Brice will never move down South. He grew up in California. He's never wanted to live anywhere else."

Logan wanted to ask her the question: *Not even for you?* But he drank from his glass instead.

"And…" Josephine felt bad for making Brice seem like her dream-killer. "I can certainly practice civil rights law in California…immigration law."

Josephine looked out the window at the clouds for a minute and then nodded as if she had just convinced herself.

"Why don't you talk for a while?" She smiled at Logan. "I've been just babbling away over here."

"Well, I think you know by now that I'm a cop," Logan said with a deadpan expression.

"Yes." She frowned playfully at him. "That much I do know."

"Hey." Logan leaned his forearms on the table between them. "All kidding aside, you aren't going to hold a grudge against me for giving you those tickets, are you?"

"No, I've never been much of a grudge holder."

"That's good…because as maid of honor and best man, I think we're going to be spending a lot of time together."

"I'm sure we will," she agreed. The thought of spending time with Logan made her want to turn on her phone and check to see if Brice had called.

No messages, no missed calls.

She couldn't believe it. He *still* hadn't called or so much as sent a text. But she kept her phone turned on this time, just in case he tried.

Logan didn't want Josephine's attention to be distracted from him or their conversation. After she checked her phone, the expression on her pretty face changed. The muscles along her jawline tightened; her lips became tense. Perhaps a less casual observer wouldn't notice these almost imperceptible changes, but he did. He noticed.

"Well, I'm glad you're a forgiving woman, or this trip could've been a real bust."

Josephine looked up from her phone. "I could really say the same about you."

"I'm not sure I follow."

"I was kind of rude to you after you gave me the tickets. You were trying to tell me who you were and probably that you were heading to the same place I was, but I cut you off."

"Trust me, I'm used to it. Nobody's happy when I hand them a ticket."

"I'm still sorry. I was just…"

"Mad at me."

"Mad at you…mad at me…mad at…" *Brice.* "…the stupid clock that said I was late!" She laughed at herself, and then asked him, "But did you really have to give me *three* tickets? I mean, come on! I really think that someone with my driving record deserved a warning."

"Your driving record is the reason I dropped the charge down from reckless driving."

Josephine frowned. "Would you have still given me all of those tickets if you knew I was Jordan's sister right away?"

"Of course."

"Seriously?"

"Enforcing the law isn't personal for me. It's my job. Most people just don't get that."

Josephine's phone rang and interrupted their conversation. "It's Brice!"

"Hi, honey. Hold on, okay?" Josephine stood up, moved out of Logan's earshot, and sat down in the last seat at the very back of the jet.

"Okay, are you there?" she asked in a lowered voice. "I'm so glad that you called…"

Head down, Josephine listened carefully to what her boyfriend called to say. After a couple of minutes, she asked in a harsh whisper, "What do you *mean* you aren't coming to the wedding?"

Chapter Three

Josephine didn't really think that Brice had deliberately tried to spoil her first homecoming in years. But that's what it *felt* like on her end. He had called specifically to tell her that he thought it was best if they took a break from their relationship. He had basically broken up with her, and left her dateless for her own twin's wedding in the span of five minutes. Brice had said what he called to say and then got off the phone. He had been between appointments when he called.

After they'd hung up, she had stared at the phone for a while, wondering what to do next. Pretty quickly, she decided it would be best if she pretended, for a while at least, that the phone call had never happened. What if this whole thing blew over in the next couple of days and she had been bemoaning their breakup to her family the entire time? Her family didn't need one extra piece of ammo against Brice. So, pretend she did…

She smiled all the way through their mini family re-
union at the Helena airport. She smiled her way through
the long ride home to Bent Tree, the family ranch. And
she smiled and laughed her way to the end of dinner and
clearing the table and loading the dishwasher. And she
didn't stop smiling and pretending until she could retreat to her third-floor bedroom. This was the bedroom
of her adolescence, the bedroom that she had shared
with Jordan. She switched on the antique Tiffany lamp
next to the door and gently pushed the door shut. The
room smelled of cedar and cinnamon, and the nostalgia
for her uncomplicated youth made her start to tear up.

She wiped the tears out of her eyes and said sternly
to herself, "Stop that!"

Josephine worked very hard not to cry while she unpacked her suitcase and carefully hung up her clothing
in the small closet. Undergarments and jeans were neatly
folded into a dresser drawer, a nice variety of shoe op-
tions was neatly lined up in the closet, and toiletries were
put away in the small en-suite bathroom. Josephine had
stowed her empty suitcase beneath the bed and began
to unpack her books.

A quick, loud knock on the door startled her. Before
she could react, the door swung open, and Jordan bar-
reled into the bedroom with the family cat, Ranger, flung
over her shoulder.

"Okay if we come in?" Jordan asked.

"I think you're already in, aren't you?"

"Good point." Barefoot, her sister sat cross-legged
on the bed and gently put Ranger down on the mattress.
Ranger, a big coal-black cat with bright golden eyes, immediately flopped onto his side and began to wash his
long, black whiskers.

"So…what's wrong, Jo?"

Josephine looked over at her sister, gave her a weak smile. She knew she had to tell her twin about Brice now; lying to Jordan was a waste of time. They had never been able to keep secrets from each other.

"Brice and I are…going through a rough patch."

Jordan moved over to one side of the bed and patted the spot next to her. "That's what I figured."

Josephine kicked off her shoes and joined her sister and Ranger on the bed. She sat cross-legged, facing her sister with Ranger sprawled out between them, belly up.

"This is just like old times, isn't it?" she asked Jordan. "Except we had two single beds in here instead of this queen-size bed."

"I had a picture of Ian from his modeling days hanging up right there." Jordan pointed to the spot just above the rolltop desk.

"And now you're marrying him, Jordy…the man of your dreams." Josephine smiled right before she felt new rash of tears starting to form.

Jordan saw the tears swimming in her eyes. "Tell me what's going on, Jo."

Josephine pressed her lips together tightly, looked away for a moment to gather her emotions before she said, "Brice called and told me that he isn't coming to the wedding. He thinks we should use our time apart this summer to reflect on our relationship in order to make a prudent decision about our future"

"Wait a minute…he *dumped* you?" Jordan's eyebrows collapsed together. "The *knuckle dragger* dumped *you*?"

"He didn't *dump* me exactly. He just wants us to reflect…"

"Oh, my *God*, Jo! Don't *defend* him!" Jordan nearly yelled those words.

Josephine jumped off the bed and shut the door. "Could you keep your voice down, please? I don't want anyone else to know! This whole thing could just blow over tomorrow."

"Why would you even *want* it to blow over?"

Josephine sat back down on the bed. "Because I love him, that's why. We've been together for over five years. I'm not just going to throw that all away just because there's a little bump in the road."

"This isn't a tiny little bump, Jo, this is a ginormous frickin' crater!"

Josephine scratched Ranger beneath his chin and on the top of his silky head. "I know you've never liked Brice, Jordy."

"I never once said that I didn't like him."

Josephine looked up at her sister. "You call him 'the knuckle dragger' more than you call him Brice."

"Fine, so I don't like him. But that's just because he thinks he's better than us, Jo. He thinks he's better than *you*, with his family money and country club and connections to *Beverly Hills*, like any of us could give a rat's behind."

"I know that's how he seems to you, to all of you, but do you really think that I'd be with him for five years if he wasn't a good guy?" Josephine said pointedly. "There's a lot more to Brice than any of you really know because none of you have given him an honest chance. Dad's always so *stiff* around him and Mom has refused to warm up to him just because I decided…" She put her hand on her heart. "*I decided* to spend the

Christmas after Daniel died with his family instead of coming home."

"Well, Brice knew your brother had just died. It was stupid of him to even invite you to his parents' *La Jolla beach house* in the first place."

Josephine sighed from frustration. "Just promise you won't tell anyone. Okay? If they need to know, I'll tell everyone myself."

Jordan pretended to lock her lips and toss the key over her shoulder. Her sister stood up, wrapped her arms around her shoulders, and gave her a tight squeeze.

"Now, come on, let's go downstairs. There's no sense in you sitting up here by yourself moping, especially if you don't want anyone to pick up on the fact that something's wrong," Jordan said. "Besides, nothing's better for heartbreak than family."

As it turned out, Jordan was right. Spending time with her family had helped get her mind off Brice's sudden, and unexpected, desire to end their relationship. And the plans for Jordan's wedding were the best kind of distraction for her. Her mom had turned the family library into "Wedding Central," and once she went back downstairs, she spent hours in the library with Jordan and her mom looking through all of the wedding regalia. She was blissfully surrounded by cake toppers and invitations, seating charts and stacks of RSVPs that needed to be answered. There were scrapbooks filled with all of the selections that had been made for the wedding and Josephine immersed herself in looking through each and every one. She spent hours, laughing and talking with her sister and her mother, and she was stunned when she realized that Brice had barely crossed her mind.

But afterward, when she was alone in bed, in the dark, all she could think of *was* Brice. Her mind just kept on going over the last several months of her relationship over and over again. Had there been signs that she hadn't seen? Red flags that she had willfully ignored? Yes, he had been distant and unavailable, but he had just been handed the biggest case of his young career. This case could make or break his career in the field of environmental law. He needed to be focused and she had understood. But now that he had suggested that they take a "break" from their relationship and left her without a wedding date, the idea that his withdrawal from their relationship was only work-related was no longer a plausible explanation. So, what was it?

"Another woman?" Josephine queried quietly aloud. *It feels like another woman.*

That's what her head was saying. That was what her gut was saying. But her heart just couldn't accept it just yet. Another woman meant that everything that they had been working toward together for years was over. Done. A horrible waste of time for the both of them.

Knowing that she wasn't going to be able to go to sleep with all of these questions buzzing around in her brain, Josephine got out of bed and quickly pulled on some sweatpants and matching sweatshirt. Josephine tiptoed down the wooden stairs and she was careful to avoid the creaky boards. Life on the ranch started before dawn, so bedtime was early. Chances were, she'd have the downstairs to herself, which was exactly what she wanted. At the bottom of the stairwell, by the dim light streaming in from the library lamp that was always left on, Josephine stopped to straighten the picture of her brother, Daniel, in his Army uniform. She had three older brothers, but everyone knew that Daniel had been her favorite. After he was killed in Iraq, it was hard for her to imagine the ranch without him. It still was.

After one last look at her brother's portrait, Josephine continued her quiet route to the front door. The front door was always unlocked, so she slowly turned the knob, and pulled the door free from the frame. Once that was accomplished, she carefully pushed the squeaky screen door open a crack, slipped through, and stepped out onto the front porch. She'd started suffering from insomnia when she was in high school, and when she couldn't sleep, she had always found her way to the giant rocking chairs on the front porch. Still holding the screen door open, she closed her eyes and breathed in the cool, fresh Montana air. She had missed that smell; it was clean and crisp.

"You're not out here alone." A male voice in the dark made her jump.

Startled, Josephine let go of the screen door handle and it slammed back into place. Her heart gave one hard thud in her chest; she placed her hand over her heart.

"Sorry," Logan said in a loud whisper. "I didn't want to scare you."

"Your attempt to not scare me *scared* me," Josephine whispered back.

"Sorry," he repeated.

Crossing her arms over her chest, Josephine hesitated for a second before she decided to join him. It wasn't ideal; she wanted to be alone. But she wanted to sit outside in her favorite rocking chair more than she wanted to go back upstairs. She sat down in the rocking chair, glad that Logan wasn't occupying it, and sighed more loudly than she had intended.

"Taking a break from your studies?" Logan asked.
Obviously, he's going to insist on talking.

"Insomnia. Chronic."

"It takes me a while to get comfortable in a strange bed."

Josephine nodded silently.

"I wanted to get to bed early so I could get up early to hike. I suppose I'm going to have to plan on covering less ground tomorrow."

For the first time since she had joined him, Josephine turned her head his way. "You like to hike?"

Logan moved over to the rocking chair next to her so he could talk to her in a quiet voice. "Hiking, mountain climbing, rock climbing, anything outdoors…if you can name it, I'm probably into it. How about you? Growing up in a place like this, you must love to hike."

"I used to hike all over these mountains when I was a kid. No matter how old I get, I think I'll always love these mountains the most."

"Well…" Logan stood up. "I think I'm gonna give sleep another try. But if you want to join me, I'm thinking about heading out around seven, seven-thirty."

"There's so much to do around here with the wedding. But thank you, though."

"Sure." Logan headed down the porch stairs, using the light of the moon to light his footing. At the bottom of the steps, Logan paused to look back at her.

"If you change your mind, I wouldn't mind the company."

"I'll let you know. Good night, Logan."

"Good night." Hands in his pockets, Logan strolled in the moonlight the short distance back to Tyler's bachelor cabin.

She had wanted him to go; she had been relieved when he got up to leave. But now that she was alone on the porch, and alone with her thoughts, Josephine suddenly regretted that Logan had left. He had distracted her, temporarily, from her melancholy and now it was back. Instead of staying on the porch, as she intended, she crept back inside, popped some over-the-counter sleeping aids, and took a steaming hot bath. If she could just get herself to sleep, if she could just *demand* that her body go to sleep, things would most likely appear less crappy in the morning. Josephine got into bed with that hope. She punched her pillows, kicked at her sheets and blanket, and finally, stiffly, flopped onto her back, hugged one of her pillows to her chest, and closed her eyes. She had already made up her mind that she was going to stay right where she was until she fell asleep. Even if it took all night.

The next morning, Josephine wasn't surprised when she awakened before the alarm went off. Even with insomnia, she had always been an early riser. Ranger had meowed at her bedroom door until she had finally relented and let him in. Why he had picked her, she couldn't be sure, but he had curled his body around the top of her head and she had fallen asleep to the rhythmic sound of his loud purring. After she rubbed the sleep out of her eyes, Josephine sat up slowly, scooped Ranger into her arms, and hugged him. He started to purr again, and she kissed him on the head before she set him gently on the bed. She could hear her family already stirring downstairs and she wanted to join them.

"Let's go see what everyone is up to," she said to Ranger.

Josephine got dressed quickly and headed downstairs.

"Good morning." Josephine walked into the kitchen with Ranger trotting along beside her.

The smell of homemade biscuits, sizzling butter, sweet bacon, and eggs permeated the kitchen. Mom was at the industrial-grade stove, frying up more eggs. Her father, Hank, was in his usual seat at the head of the long rectangular table that could seat up to twenty ranch workers if necessary. The family dog, a German shepherd named Ilsa, was sitting to Hank's left, patiently waiting for her father to sneak her a piece of bacon. Tyler was at his father's right hand, guzzling down a large mug of coffee loaded with cream and sugar. Logan sat to Tyler's right, quietly eating his breakfast. It was strange for her to see someone else occupying what had been Daniel's favored seat at the table. Logan nodded his head and smiled at her; she gave him a quick smile in return.

"Good morning, sweetheart, did you sleep well?" Barbara Brand tilted her head a bit so her daughter could give her their customary kiss.

"Once I finally fell asleep, I slept like a rock." Josephine wrapped her arms around her mom's shoulders from behind, gave her a quick hug, and a kiss on the cheek.

No matter what time in the morning, Barbara was always put together. Her mom smelled faintly of her signature perfume; her hair, blond streaked with silver, was pulled back off her classically pretty face into a chignon, and her makeup was light and flawlessly applied. The woman never gave up. She had lived with dirty cowboys and cows for over forty years, but she had refused to let go of her sophisticated, big-city Chicago roots. Her mottos were Simplicity Is Elegance and A Woman

Can Be Stylish Anywhere. And she lived those mottos on a daily basis.

"Orange juice is on the table. Scrambled or fried?" Barbara pointed to the eggs with her spatula.

"I think I'm just going to grab coffee and a banana." Josephine put her hands lightly on her mom's shoulders. "Can I help?"

"No, honey, I'm just doing my thing. Go spend some time with Dad before he disappears for the day." Barbara started to flip the eggs over one by one.

Next, Josephine greeted her father with a hug and a kiss.

"Mornin', Princess. You're up with the rooster." Her father squeezed her hand affectionately.

Henry "Hank" Brand had Montana ranching in his blood. His family had owned the Bent Tree Cattle Ranch for four generations. Raising cattle was what Hank loved to do; he was in his early sixties, but he was tall and lean and could still sit straight in the saddle with the youngest ranch hands. He had thick silver hair, usually hidden beneath a cowboy hat, and he had bright blue trademark Brand eyes, deeply set, that stood out in contrast to the tanned skin of his narrow face.

"Sit right here next to me." Hank leaned over and pulled the chair out for his daughter to join him.

Josephine grabbed a cup of coffee and then headed back to the table. Before she sat down, she hugged Ilsa around the neck; the shepherd was definitely starting to show her age. Ilsa was graying around her muzzle and eyes. Josephine took the seat next to her father and reached for a large ripe banana from a bowl of fruit. Tyler stopped chewing for a second to smile at her with closed lips; he nodded to the pitcher of fresh-squeezed orange juice. She held out her glass for Tyler to fill it for her.

"So what you were saying, Logan, is that we might be able to relocate the chapel?" Hank pushed his plate forward and reached for his mug full of steaming black coffee.

"I don't know why we're even discussing this." Barbara walked back over to the table, her hands resting firmly on her hips. "We aren't changing the venue for the wedding. I've been killing myself for over a year with all of these arrangements. We've paid the deposit, the invitations have been sent out…" Everyone in the kitchen, including the dog, was focused on Barbara now. "St. Peter's is where all of my children were baptized, St. Peter's is where Dan is buried, and St. Peter's is where the wedding is going to be held!"

Hank reached for his wife's hand. "Barb, we're just talking about relocating the chapel. Jordan knows that the chapel is out of the question for the wedding."

"Oh, I missed that part." Before Barb turned back to the stove, she pointed to her son. "Tyler, how many times have I asked you to *not* to feed Ranger at the table?"

Josephine looked across the table at her brother; Ranger was sitting on Tyler's lap waiting for a morsel to come his way. Tyler winked at her and smiled, but didn't move Ranger.

"I haven't been up to the chapel in years." Josephine remembered playing wedding there with Jordan when they were girls. "Are you really thinking about moving the chapel, Dad? How? And where would you put it?"

Great-grandpa Brand had been a full-time rancher and a part-time preacher. He'd built a small chapel on the ranch with his own hands, and had a small congregation that would come on Sunday morning to hear him preach. It had sat abandoned, unused, for decades.

"I don't really know." Hank snuck Ilsa a full strip of bacon from his plate. "I haven't been up there in years. I couldn't tell you if it's even still standing."

"It's standing," Tyler said. "But it's rough. Real rough."

"I'd be willing to take a look at it for you, sir," Logan offered. "My uncle's a contractor. He had me framing houses before I could drive. I could take some pictures and get my uncle take a look at them."

Hank stood up and grabbed his hat off the back of his chair. "I'd appreciate that."

Ranger hopped down to the ground when Tyler stood up and grabbed his hat as well. "I can take him up there so he can get a look around."

"No, I need you supervising the work on the north fence today." Hank grabbed his plate and utensils, stacked them in the sink, and then kissed his wife.

It hit her out of the blue, but the only thing Josephine wanted to do with her morning was see the chapel. She didn't want to spend the morning cooped up with a bunch of textbooks. She wanted to get out in the fresh air, get out into the sunlight, and get her blood pumping by hiking her way up to the ninety-year-old chapel.

"Mom? Jordan's not going to be ready to tackle wedding stuff until after noon. If you don't need me, I could take Logan up to see the chapel."

"That's fine, honey. Just make sure you take plenty of water and bug spray." Her mother never took a break from being her mother.

Josephine looked at Logan. "If you don't mind...I'll take you to the chapel."

Logan had been sitting across the table from Josephine, trying not to stare at her. There was just something about her that got his attention and *held* it. Would he *mind* spending the morning hiking in the mountains with the most beautiful woman he'd seen in a long time?

Heck, no!

Logan did his best *not* to look like a kid who had just been handed the keys to the candy store when he casually said to Josephine, "No, I don't mind."

Chapter Four

Josephine quickly changed into a pair of denim cutoff shorts and hiking boots, and layered a sweatshirt over a Berkeley Law T-shirt. She grabbed sunglasses, a baseball cap, and raced down the stairs. She deliberately left her cell phone behind. This was her time to take a break from her worries over her relationship with Brice. This was her first full day home at the ranch and it seemed sacrilegious *not* to at least make the attempt to enjoy it.

"Ready?" Logan was waiting for her.

"Ready." Josephine hopped down the porch stairs to meet him.

Logan liked the way Josephine's face was lit up with excitement. He had no doubt that the excitement was related to the hike and seeing the chapel, but he couldn't stop himself from hoping that perhaps spending time with him factored into that equation.

"Lead the way, boss." Logan lifted his heavy rucksack onto his shoulders.

They walked along a well-worn dirt road that would lead them up the mountain to her great-grandfather's chapel. Before they reached the tree line at the base of the mountain, the early morning sun was heating up the bright blue, cloudless sky. By the time they reached tree line, Josephine was ready to shed her outer layer of clothing.

"This road will take us about three-quarters of the way up this mountain." She wrapped her sweatshirt around her hips and put her hat back on. "There's an incredible view of the continental divide once you reach the peak. You've got to be sure to check that out while you're here, but you'll have to get there on foot or on horseback. Do you ride?"

Logan nodded. "All my life."

"Well…" Josephine slid the sunglasses back into place. "Anytime you want to ride, just let London know. She's the intern working in the foaling barn. She'll make sure there's a horse saddled up for you."

Together, side by side, they walked along the gravel and dirt road that followed a winding stream up the mountain. Although she had known him for only a very short time, it wasn't awkward hiking alone with Logan. Out of his uniform, he wasn't uptight. Their conversation was easy, and right when a lull was about to occur, Logan would ask her another question about the history of the ranch. She couldn't stop herself from thinking that Brice had never shown this much interest in her family's history. Even though she hadn't really paid much attention to that before today. But with Logan's genuine interest as a comparison, it was pretty hard to ignore.

"Do you mind if we take a quick break?" she asked when they reached the halfway point.

Josephine found a large boulder near the stream embankment and sat down. She closed her eyes for a minute to enjoy fully the sounds of the mountains. It seemed so quiet when they were walking and talking, but right now she could hear how loud the water flowing over the rocks in the stream sounded.

"Thirsty?" Logan, kneeling nearby, had opened his rucksack. He held out a bottle of water to her, which she accepted.

She drank the water slowly, taking some time to catch her breath. Logan downed his water, stuffed the empty bottle back into his bag, and then stripped his T-shirt off. Beneath it was a ribbed tank top that clung to his chest and stomach. For a second, Josephine found herself mindlessly staring at Logan. He wasn't tall; she typically dated tall men. In fact, when she stood next to him in heels, she was a little taller than he was.

But on the other hand, he was built like Michelangelo's *David*. His body was incredible. She'd never seen anything like it in real life. His shoulders, his biceps, his chest, were covered with thick, defined muscle. His waist was tapered and she could actually see the ripples of his abdominal muscles through the ribbed material. Logan didn't have a six-pack—he had an *eight*-pack. In particular, she was fascinated by the large tattoo of a dark gray wolf that covered a large portion of his upper left arm and chest. Part of the tattoo was obscured by his tank top, and Josephine wished she could move the material over and take a closer look at the design. It looked like beautiful work. Knowing that she needed to stop staring at the man, she looked at the stream instead. But, she could still see him out of the corner of her eye as he wiped the sweat off his face, neck, and arms with his T-shirt.

After a minute, she stood up and brushed the dirt off the seat of her shorts. "I'm over here huffing and puffing and you've barely broken a sweat."

Logan rolled up his T-shirt and packed it back into the rucksack. "I spend a lot of time indoor rock climbing."

"It shows." This was blurted out without thought. Josephine inwardly cringed as she extended her empty bottle to him.

He smiled at her as he held out his hand for her bottle. She was genuinely relieved when he didn't latch on to her comment and run with it. He just zipped up his bag, slung it back onto his shoulders, and adjusted the straps for comfort.

"Ready?" he asked.

"Yep." Now that she had caught her breath, she was eager to reach the chapel. So many years had passed by since she had laid eyes on her childhood haunt. What would it be like to see it now, through the eyes of an adult?

"There's a fork in the road up ahead," she told him. "If you take this road to the right, it will take you to a cave that my grandfather found."

"A cave?"

She sidestepped a dip in the road. "It's incredible. But it's hard to get into. You basically have to crawl on your back along this narrow tunnel that leads to the main chamber. The main chamber is huge—completely dark. Archaeologists have studied our cave for years. There are areas all along the sides of the main area where they believe that prehistoric humans lived. And they ended up finding a lot of artifacts in the main chamber and some of the smaller chambers."

"I'll have to check it out."

"I don't like the crawling part so much… It's a little claustrophobic. But once you get inside, you feel like you've been transported back in time. I haven't been there in ages, but I can still remember how cold it was inside the cave."

At the top of a hill, they reached the fork in the road. She stopped for a minute to catch her breath; she had put in hundreds of hours on the elliptical machine, and the climb was still tough. The change in altitude, the thinner air, impacted her mild case of asthma. Next time she came up here, she'd have to remember her inhaler.

"Up that way is the cave…" She pointed to the right.

"I suppose this isn't the day for that?"

"I really need to get back before noon. There's still a lot that needs to get done for the wedding. But, you can head up there after we see the chapel, if you want."

Logan shifted his rucksack on his back to a more comfortable position. "We'll see."

In actuality, he didn't intend to separate from her. This was her ranch, and she knew the territory better than he did, but he had a protective nature. He wouldn't feel right not seeing her safely back to the house.

"It's not too far now," Josephine said as they started up a new hill. Her thigh muscles were burning from the hike and she couldn't believe how much protesting her body was doing. When she had been a little girl, she could run up and down these hills without any trouble at all. Now, it was taking all of her strength, physical and mental, to hike to the chapel without taking a ton of minibreaks. If Logan hadn't been with her, she would have taken several breaks already. But since he was pressing on, she was pressing on.

At the bottom of another steep hill, the final hill that would lead them to the plateau where her great-grandfather had built his chapel, Josephine paused. Her face felt hot and wet with perspiration. She used the sleeve of her sweatshirt to wipe the sweat from her face and then prepared to tackle the last leg of this impromptu hike.

"Doing okay?" Logan stood beside her patiently.

She nodded. "The altitude is getting to me."

"You've been setting a really tough pace for this hike," he said. "Why don't we slow it down a bit?"

Hands on her hips, bending forward slightly, trying to catch her breath again, Josephine looked at him, surprised. "I've been setting the pace?"

He nodded his head "yes."

Josephine laughed a breathy laugh, and then coughed. "And here I've been blaming it on you!"

Logan laughed with her. "No. I've had to work to keep up."

"You're kidding?" Josephine laughed again with a shake of her head. "Do you mean that I feel a little like I'm going to pass out and I've done it to myself?"

Logan's smiled faded as he took a step toward her. "You feel light-headed?"

"A little. It's no big deal. Asthma."

"Here…" He pointed to a flat boulder on the side of the road. "I think you should sit down."

"The chapel is right up that hill. I'll rest when I get up there."

"How long has the chapel been there?"

"A hundred years."

Logan put his hand on her shoulder to guide her toward the boulder. "Then, chances are it'll still be there thirty minutes from now."

It was a point that she couldn't argue, so she walked over to the boulder and let him help her down to a sitting position. She crossed her legs and gave herself permission to rest.

One knee on the ground, Logan knelt in front of her and opened his rucksack. He held out two high-energy protein bars for her to see.

"Take your pick."

She chose the peanut-butter bar and gratefully accepted another bottle of water.

"What else do you have in that thing?" she asked when he joined her on the boulder. "It's like you're carrying a mini convenience store on your back."

He opened the wrapper of his bar with his teeth. "Did you see the movie *127 Hours*?"

"Uh-uh…" She wished she had time for movies, but she didn't.

"It was about a rock climber who had to cut off his own arm."

"Oh!" She nodded. "I remember that—the guy in Utah, right?"

"As a rock climber, first, it kind of scared the crap out of me, to be honest. But second, it reminded me that I have to be prepared because, if a freak accident like that could happen to that guy, a freak accident could happen to me."

Then he asked, "Feeling better?"

"Much." After eating the protein bar and taking a moment to rest, the light-headed feeling had passed.

"Ready to get back to it?"

Josephine nodded. "Sure."

Logan stood up and offered her his hand, which she accepted.

"Thank you for talking me into taking a break—and feeding me."

"Anytime." He hoisted the heavy backpack onto his shoulders.

She had enjoyed it, as well. Sitting with Logan on that boulder, without another soul in sight, had been perfectly comfortable. It had taken her months to feel comfortable around Brice; he had always made her feel so nervous because he was so brilliant with the law. If she were to be honest with herself, sometimes Brice still made her feel a little anxious whenever they got into a conversation about California statutes or federal law. But with Logan, she was at total ease—not a single nerve in sight.

What did that mean?

Josephine forced her brain to stop trying to unravel meaningless life riddles, and refocus on finishing her trek up the steep hill. She leaned slightly forward, bent her knees, ignored the burning in her thighs and lungs, and willed her body to finish the last half of the hill quickly. At the top of the hill, Josephine threw back her head and let out a loud whoop to celebrate her accomplishment.

"I made it!" she exclaimed happily.

Logan joined her at the top of the final hill. She was glad to see that he was finally winded, too.

"Now, that felt good..." He wiped the sweat off his brow with the back of his forearm. He smiled at her. "You're a maniac."

Pleased, she asked, "I am?" No one had ever called

her that before. Cautious and tenacious, yes. Maniac?
Never.

"I nearly had to sprint up that hill just to keep up with
you." He was impressed with her. "I'd really love to take
you rock climbing one day."

For a moment, they both considered what he had just
said. It sounded like he had asked her out on a date.

Knowing that she had a serious boyfriend, Logan
added, "You and Brice…"

"I think I can safely say that it would be a definite
'no' for Brice." Brice was an avid sportsman. And he
was very skilled at many things: fencing, sailing, golf-
ing. But rock climbing? That wouldn't turn out well for
anyone involved.

"It's not for everyone," he agreed, walking beside her
through a small clearing to the edge of a patch of trees
and overgrown brush.

"There it is!" Josephine pushed some branches out of
her path and stepped over a fallen log. "See?"

"That is too cool." Logan looked through the branches
of the trees and spotted the old chapel, tucked away in
the hillside.

He pulled a small machete out of his rucksack. "Let
me get in front of you so I can cut a path for us."

She shook her head, an amused smile on her face.
"Really? You brought a machete?"

"Like I told you, I need to be prepared. I never know
when I might have to perform an emergency amputa-
tion." He stepped in front of her and started whacking
away at the branches.

"We'll have none of that, sir." She hung back, far
away from the sharp blade.

Logan seemed to relish clearing a path for them,

and in no time at all, they were standing in front of the chapel. They stood together, silently and reverently, in front of the structure that her ancestor had built a hundred years before. It was a small building—much smaller than she remembered. But, she supposed, everything looked smaller when you looked at it again as an adult. And yet, it was just as magical as she remembered.

"It looks like a little hobbit house, doesn't it?" She asked him quietly. She didn't know why she was whispering—it just felt right.

Logan put away the machete. "The construction is incredible. It still looks solid as a rock."

The chapel was the size of a modern day one-car garage, with a steeple roof, stone foundation, and a curved, heavy wooden door. The shallow stone steps leading up to the chapel door were covered in moss, decomposing leaves, and twigs.

Josephine ran her hand over the pitted wood of the chapel door. "I always loved this door—I can't really believe that it's still here…still on its hinges."

Logan checked the hinges. "They're rusted through. If you want to go inside, it's going to take some brute force."

"I'm going in." There wasn't any scenario in the equation that didn't include her going inside the chapel.

Together, they used their body weight and strength to force the door open. Logan slammed the side of his body into the wood, while she used her hands to push. Finally, after several attempts of prying the hinges free, there was a loud sound and the door cracked open.

"Keep pushing!" Logan leaned harder into the door, using his feet to brace himself in place.

The top door hinge broke under the pressure, popped off, and flew over her shoulder.

"Whoa!" She ducked to the side. "That was close!"

"You all right?"

"Yeah…it just missed me. Can we get in?"

"Almost." He gave the door one last hard shove with his body and pushed it open wide enough for them to squeeze through.

Logan stepped inside the dusty, cobweb-laden chapel first. It was dirty, and there were signs that animals had been inside of the structure, but it appeared to be safe.

When she stepped inside of the chapel, it was like stepping back in time. Her heart felt it…her brain felt it…for just a split-second, she was transported to her childhood. This was the enchanted place where she had played and dreamed with her twin. They would spend from sunrise to sunset up on this mountain, perfectly content acting out every fantasy they could imagine.

"Look—only one of the stained glass windows broke." Josephine slowly walked along the narrow aisle that led up to a pulpit hand-carved by her father's grandfather.

On either side of the aisle, roughly hewn benches were tipped onto their sides. Originally, there had been four benches on either side of the aisle. Now, there were only five benches left. Birds had flown through the broken window and had made nests up in the rafters. Much like the chapel itself, the nests seemed to have been abandoned long ago.

"What do you think?" she asked him.

"I love this place," Logan said immediately. His eyes were taking inventory. He'd spent a lot of time on jobs with his uncle and he had been personally involved with moving older structures.

The moment she reached the pulpit, she started to brush the dirt and leaves off of it. She could see herself, so clear was the memory, standing behind the pulpit pretending to preach to an enthralled congregation.

Her fingers found what they were searching for: her initials, carved into the top of the pulpit. "Can it be moved?"

On the other side of the pulpit, he looked up at the tin roof and the beams holding it in place. He nodded slowly, thoughtfully. "Yes. It can."

"You're serious."

"It can be done," Logan said definitively.

Her mind started to whirl with ideas. "If we moved it closer to the ranch, we could actually restore it!"

"Absolutely." He would love to have a hand in restoring the chapel.

Face-to-face, with only the pulpit between them, they stood smiling at each other as if they had just uncovered a buried treasure. Josephine, exactly at that moment, noticed Logan's eyes. Yes, she had seen his eyes before. But, she hadn't really noticed how incredibly beautiful they were—such a dark, rich brown that they reminded her of expensive black satin.

"What?" He asked her, in a half curious, half amused manner.

His single-word question snapped her out of it—she had been unintentionally staring into his eyes. Once she realized that she had been mindlessly ogling him, she started to laugh.

"Sorry—I was just thinking about something from when I was a kid."

"What's that?"

"When I was…oh, I don't know…seven or eight…"

Josephine walked out from behind the pulpit and joined Logan where he was standing.

"I used to stand in this exact spot and pretend that I was getting married. Jordan and I took turns officiating the wedding and being the bride..." Josephine laughed softly and looked over at him. "You standing here just reminded me of that. I haven't thought of that in years. And, of course, that was before I discovered Gloria Steinem when I was thirteen and swore off marriage entirely."

"But, Gloria Steinem did eventually get married," Logan said thoughtfully.

Brow wrinkled, Josephine asked, "How do you even *know* that?"

"Hey, I'll have you know I'm more than just a pretty face. I'm current with the cause, equal pay for equal work. The Lilly Ledbetter Law."

Josephine laughed. "I hate to say this out loud, but I wouldn't take you for a feminist sympathizer."

"That's okay. I know that I don't exactly fit the image of a typical feminist. I'm a cop who looks like a muscle-head. But my mom was raised on *Ms.* magazine—so I pretty much had the chauvinist trained out of me at an early age." Logan smiled at the thought and pulled out a professional-grade Nikon camera from his bag. "Let's grab these shots so we can get you back by noon."

"Sure." Josephine checked her watch with a nod. "Where do you want to start?"

Chapter Five

They both had similar work styles—slow, methodical, and thorough. Together, they captured detailed shots of the interior of the chapel, as well as the exterior and surrounding landscape. She had helped Logan take measurements before they started their hike down the mountain. Both of them were so excited about the prospect of moving the chapel that they discussed it nonstop all the way back down the mountain. By the time that they reached the gate, which signaled that the final leg of the journey was complete, it seemed to Josephine that the two of them had bonded. On the round trip to and from the chapel, she had unexpectedly made a connection with Logan. He felt like a friend.

"Well..." Logan paused at the end of the path that led to her brother's cabin. "I'm going to send my uncle these pictures and measurements so I can report back to Hank."

Josephine nodded toward her sister, who had set up her easels and paints on the porch and was painting a new picture for her next gallery show. "It looks like Jordan is waiting for me."

They parted ways. After he had taken a few steps away from her, Logan stopped and turned to look at her.

"Hey…" he called out to her.

Josephine slowed down and glanced back at him.

"Thanks for being my guide today."

She smiled a small smile. "I enjoyed it."

For a second time, they parted ways and Josephine had an odd feeling in the pit of her stomach as she approached her sister. Jordan looked tense and irritated, when she normally looked happy when she painted. She was also, Josephine noted, biting on her lower lip, which was what she did whenever she was upset or ticked off.

"Hey." Josephine slowly climbed the stairs to the front porch.

"Hey…" Jordan put down her paintbrush and moved to the porch swing. "How'd the chapel look?"

Josephine perched on the porch railing opposite the swing. "It's pretty rough on the inside, but salvageable. Logan believes the structure's sound—you know, Dad has it in his head to move it."

"Mom told me. Cool idea."

"Logan's pretty certain that it can be moved." Josephine wrapped her arm around the wooden post to keep her balance.

"He's a great guy, right? He's been a huge part of our support system."

Her sister was stalling. Whatever was on her mind, it had to be bad. Outspoken Jordan didn't often beat around the bush.

"So, have we done enough small talking yet?" Josephine asked her twin pointedly.

Her sister stared at her and they didn't need words between them. A couple of seconds later, Jordan frowned, shook her head, and pulled her phone out of the front pocket of her shorts. Silently, Jordan looked down at the phone before she looked at her.

"I saw something on Instagram this morning."

Josephine wasn't sure where this was heading, but her stomach already didn't like it. There was an uncomfortable, unusual, anxious quivering in her belly. It was if her body knew something that her mind hadn't yet figured out.

"I didn't know if I should show it to you or not, but here…" Jordan uncurled her long, pale legs, stood up, and held out her phone to her.

Josephine met her sister's angry eyes and then took the phone from her. When she saw the picture on Jordan's phone, her arm tightened around the post. She hugged the post so tightly, in fact, that the wood dug painfully into her skin.

"Where was this taken? Do you know?"

"At a charity event."

She had been with Brice when he had been measured for that tuxedo, but this photograph was the first time she had seen him wear it. It fit beautifully. But then again, everything fit Brice beautifully. Nature had been very kind to him—he was tall with nice shoulders and golden-boy good looks. The woman beside him—her arm linked with his, her hand on his sleeve, her body leaned intimately into his—was stunning. She had shoulder-length dark hair, flawless olive skin, and full red lips. Josephine wished she could put her into the "bimbo" category, but this woman had intelligent eyes and a classic, elegant style.

She handed the phone back to Jordan. "Well, I suppose we know why he's not coming to the wedding."

"That's it?" Jordan slipped the phone back into her pocket.

Josephine slid off the railing and tugged the legs of her shorts down. "That's it."

"I was right to tell you, I think," her sister said defensively.

"Of course you were." She hugged Jordan to reassure her. "I'm going to go freshen up and then we'll work on the wedding, okay?"

"Wait a minute, Jo. Why are you acting like a Stepford Wife?" her sister asked with a shake of her head. "You should be really pissed right now, and the fact that you're not is kind of freakin' me out…"

"I'm not going to let Brice ruin the only summer I've had off in years," Josephine replied. "He apparently wants someone else. Me being angry won't change that, will it?"

"Well, then I'll be pissed off for the both of us." Jordan scowled. "If he was here right now, I'd sock him right in his stupid aristocratic beak!"

Jordan ran interference for her with their mom while she escaped to the sanctuary of her third-floor bedroom. Once inside of her room, she went to the bathroom and closed that door, too. She needed as much of a barrier between her and the world as she could muster. She sat down on the edge of the claw-footed tub and just sat there, staring at a hairline crack in the porcelain pedestal sink. It was strange—she didn't really feel angry or sad or jealous. There was a burning in her stomach and a burning behind her eyes, but she didn't need to cry.

Was she in shock? Was that it? Or had she known, at some primordial level, that he had recently lost interest in her?

"That's more like it…" she said aloud.

And who was this woman who had taken her spot at Brice's side?

Not seeing any sense in speculating about the picture when she could just call him and ask, Josephine left the bathroom, turned on her phone, and sat down at the desk. His cell phone went straight to voicemail; his secretary took a message. So, she called his private office number. She never called that number, respecting Brice's wishes that she would only use it if there were an emergency. This qualified, in her opinion.

"Hello?" He sounded good. Happy.

"It's me, Brice."

There was a long pause, followed by a chair squeak. Josephine imagined him spinning his chair around so the back of his chair was facing the people who were undoubtedly sitting on the other side of his desk.

"Josie…"

She hated it when he called her that. He was the only one who did.

"Are you okay?"

The burning in her stomach became hotter, more intense. "I'm fine."

Another pause, then he said. "I'm in the middle of something here. Let me call you back in a bit."

"Oh, sure." It was work to keep her tone light. "But, before you go, I just wanted to tell you how handsome you looked in your tuxedo last night."

She was being snarky and sarcastic and it felt…*great*.

The chair squeaked again and she heard Brice say to whomever was in his office, "I need to take this call. Let me catch up with you in fifteen."

Brice waited a second or two before he said, "I was afraid this was going to happen. I wanted to wait until you got back to tell you about Caroline."

"I think you should tell me now."

Caroline Santiago, he explained, had recently joined the firm. She was an environmental lawyer who was working on the same case. Meetings turned into lunches, which turned into dinners, and dinners turned into interest on both of their parts. But Caroline refused to date him because she knew he was involved. So, Brice decided to become uninvolved with her.

"Do you…love her?" She couldn't believe how rapidly her heart was beating. It was pumping hard like she had just sprinted for a quarter mile.

"I don't know. Maybe."

Maybe? *Maybe?* The first flush of anger broke through the numbness.

"You haven't been sleeping with the both of us, have you? I think I have the right to know if I need to make an appointment with my doctor for an STD screen."

"No. God. *No*, Josie. You know me better than that. We haven't slept together…"

There was an unspoken "yet" at the end of his sentence. They both knew it, and she couldn't allow herself to ignore it.

"You know…" she said much more calmly than she felt inside. "I've known you for five years, Brice. *Five years*. And, for the first time in all of those years, the only thing I can think to say to you is 'goodbye.'"

"Josephine…I didn't plan this. Lightning struck. But, I always want to be able to count you as one of my friends."

"Goodbye, Brice."

"Hey, Mom, how's it going?" Josephine emerged from her room as night was falling.

"Hi, sweetheart. Everyone missed you at dinner." Barb was sitting in the study, opening a new stack of RSVPs. "Did you get all of your studying done?"

She actually had gotten quite a bit of studying done. She had always had the ability to concentrate in a crisis. "It put a dent in it, at least. Where is everybody?"

"They're all out at the campfire toasting marshmallows and smoking your father's cigars." Her mom picked up her reading glasses and slipped them on.

"You aren't supposed to know about the cigars."

Her mom looked at her over the rim of her glasses. "I've been married to your father for four decades, sweetie. There isn't anything that man does that I don't know about. But when you're married, sometimes you just have to let the other person breathe. Even if it means that the breathing they're doing includes cigar smoke."

Josephine laughed before she asked, "Do you need help?"

"No, honey, I've got this all under control. Why don't you go out there and show those boys how a real pro toasts marshmallows?"

Josephine strolled along the gravel drive that led to the permanent fire pit. All of her life, and as far back as she could remember, her family had gathered around a campfire. More than anything, she had looked forward to spending time with Brice and her family by the bonfire. But that just wasn't meant to be. He didn't love her anymore. He didn't want her anymore. And she had spent the last several hours trying to adjust to a new normal. Brice had been her first love—her first lover—and she had believed that he was her future. It was difficult to be so wrong.

"Hey! Sissy!" Tyler shouted from across the fire. "Where the heck have you been?"

"Studying." She smiled at the sight of her family gathered at the fire.

Josephine sat down on one of the tree stumps that her father had fashioned into rustic chairs years ago. Her sister handed her a roasting stick and the bag of marshmallows; she carefully put two large marshmallows on to the end of the stick before she picked the perfect spot above the fire to start browning them.

"Mine always catch on fire," Logan told her.

"It takes patience." She slowly turned the stick as one side of the marshmallows began to turn golden brown and bubble.

"Here." Josephine extended the two perfectly cooked marshmallows out to Logan.

"You sure?"

She nodded. Logan pulled the gooey, hot marshmallows off the stick and popped them into his mouth. She watched his face and waited.

"Mmm." He smiled at her. "The best I've ever had. Thank you."

"Well, don't get too impressed. This is the only thing I know how to cook."

There was a moment, when she was cooking marshmallows to share with Logan and listening to Tyler strum the guitar, that she did feel normal. Perhaps most people wouldn't like the smell of campfire and cigar smoke, but for her, it represented home. She enjoyed hearing her sister and Ian talk about their wedding and their business plans and the remodeling of their downtown San Diego penthouse. She enjoyed hearing her father and Tyler discuss the day-to-day operations of the ranch. They talked and she listened. When there was finally a lull in the conversation, Josephine set the agenda for the next topic: the chapel.

"Have you heard back from your uncle?" she asked Logan.

Logan, who was pouring some water from his bottle onto his fingers to wash off the sticky residue left by the marshmallows, nodded his head.

"I filled Hank in before you got here," he said.

"So…" she asked expectantly. "What's the verdict? Can it be moved?"

Hank stubbed out his cigar and held the unsmoked part of the cigar between his thumb and forefinger. "We can move it by rigging it up and hauling it down. But we're going to have to rustle up the right equipment and that's gonna take some time."

"Don't you think that you should at least get another opinion, Dad? No offense, Logan."

"When people want a second opinion, they go to Logan's uncle," Ian said. "If someone wants an expert opinion right off the bat, they go to Logan's uncle. He's the gold standard when it comes to moving old structures. If he says that it can be done, then it can be done."

Everyone around the campfire was quite for a moment, contemplating Ian's words. Then her father spoke.

"I believe Logan wouldn't lead us astray on this. You've seen the chapel—you've seen the terrain. What do you think, son? Can the chapel be moved or should we just scrap the idea?"

Josephine couldn't stop herself from frowning. It was an immediate, unavoidable response.

Son?

She quickly looked between Logan and her father. Her father was a cautious man. He didn't just embrace people wholeheartedly without their proving their worth, and he certainly didn't trust them with decisions about the ranch on a whim. Hank had only met Logan *yesterday* and he'd already taken him into his confidence and was calling him *son?*

What the heck?

"It can be done," Logan responded. "It's going to cost a pretty penny, but it can be done."

"Money's not a problem," Hank told Logan. "But, I think we are going to need your help to get the job done."

"Uh…*wow*! Are you really going to do it, Dad?" Jordan asked.

"If Logan's willing to take time away from his vacation, this might just be the best time to finally get it done." This was her father's answer.

"I've got no problem helping out," Logan said. "I'm used to working. I need to keep busy."

"Then, let's get it done." Tyler strummed a couple of chords on his guitar. "You know I'm in."

As the campfire died down, the conversation also ebbed. The events of the last two days with Brice, and the effort it took to pretend like nothing was wrong, suddenly made her feel bone tired. She stifled a yawn behind her hand.

"Well, family, I think it's time for me to go to bed." She stood up.

After kissing her father on the cheek and saying good-night to everyone, Josephine headed back to the house. She was a short distance from the fire pit when she heard Jordan call her name. She slowed down and waited for her twin to catch up to her, and then once they were out of earshot of the rest of the family, Jordan said, "I've been worried about you. How are you holding up?"

"I actually feel pretty numb right now." Josephine crossed her arms in front of her body. "It's not the end of the world, right? It just seems like it is."

"Did you talk to Brice?"

"Sure did."

"I figured you would. Was he straight with you, or did he try to weasel out of it?"

Josephine stopped walking, and Jordan did, as well. They stood together in a shadowy stretch of the drive-way, where the light of the fire and the lights of the house didn't reach. Under the wide, blue-black, starless sky, Josephine tried to think of a way to quickly recap her conversation with Brice, but couldn't.

"Do you mind if…" She started the sentence and Jordan finished it.

"…we talk about it tomorrow?"

In the dark, Josephine nodded.

Her twin hugged her. "We don't have to talk about it at all, if you don't want to, Jo. I just want you to know that I'm here for you. I love you."

"I love you, too." Josephine returned the hug, glad for her sister's support.

After the hug ended, she said to her sister, "I'll tell everyone tomorrow—there's no sense waiting anymore. I'm sure they'll all be happy to hear it."

"No one's going to happy that you're in pain, Jo."

Josephine breathed in deeply and then let it out quickly. "No. You're right. I know you're right. Good night."

"Okay, get some rest," Jordan agreed. "But, if you need anything, you know where to find me."

Jordan headed back to the fire and her fiancé, while she returned to the farmhouse. She had almost reached to porch steps when she heard the sound of heavy footsteps on the gravel. Someone was running toward her in the dark.

"Hey, Josephine!" Logan jogged toward her. "Hold up!"

The only thing she wanted to do at the exact moment was to go to bed. She needed to wash her face, brush her teeth, get into her comfy pajamas, crawl under the covers, and be left alone. And, for some reason, she couldn't seem to make a clean getaway.

"I was just talking to your dad and Tyler about the cave and they said that you are the resident spelunker."

"I suppose that's true," she said as she stepped onto the first porch step—one step closer to her bed.

"I'm going to head up to the cave tomorrow before plans to move the chapel get under way." Logan had followed her onto the first step. "And I wanted to know if you wanted to go with me."

The first word that came to mind was "no." And it was also the first word that tried to pop out of her mouth. But she refused to speak the word. She needed to resist the urge to retreat and force herself to forge ahead.

"What time?" she asked.

"Seven?" He seemed surprised that she said yes. That made two of them.

"Seven's good," she agreed. "If I don't see you in the kitchen, I'll meet you at the gate."

Chapter Six

The next morning, Logan greeted her at the fence and they made their way back up the mountain. She wanted to be quiet on the hike—she felt like she needed it. Normally, she would ignore her needs in favor of her companion's needs, but she felt comfortable enough with Logan to speak her truth. He didn't ask her why; he just respected her wishes and only spoke when she spoke first. At the fork in the road, they traveled to the right in order to reach the cave.

"It looks like it's trying to rain," Josephine noted. The sky was a muddy gray and there were heavy storm clouds gathering in the distance.

Logan surveyed the sky. "We should get back before it starts. I've got a couple of ponchos just in case."

After that brief exchange, Josephine turned inward again. She had awakened feeling odd. She wasn't sad—

she didn't feel angry. She felt—out of sorts. Her head ached, all of her joints burned for no apparent reason. Behind her sunglasses, her eyes were tender from crying herself to sleep. This was her first real breakup with a man she still loved, and she wasn't exactly sure *how* to work through that.

Twenty more minutes along the winding mountain path, and then Josephine pointed straight ahead.

"There's the entrance, right there in that rock face."

Logan had been happy to be spending a second morning hiking with Josephine. He knew he was in permanent friend zone, no-man's-land, but he didn't see any reason why he couldn't enjoy the company of a beautiful, intelligent woman when crossing the line was already off the table. He liked her as a person, and during their second hike together, the silences between them weren't uncomfortable at all.

"I've gotta confess, I've been thinking about this place ever since you told me about it," he replied. He'd had this cave on the brain since yesterday. The idea of being able to visit an archaeological site intrigued him. He was about to enter a place where prehistoric man, and woman, had made their homes.

"I don't blame you. It's an amazing place. I remember when a crew from *National Geographic* arrived to photograph our cave. I was convinced that we were famous."

Logan noticed that she smiled, just a little, for the first time that day. He sensed that something was bothering her—there was a change in her from their trip to the chapel—but he didn't know her well enough to inquire. The best he could do was to respect her wish to hike in relative silence.

"Is that a lock?" he asked, concerned.

Josephine pulled her key chain out of her front pocket, held up an old brass key. "I never took the key off my key chain."

Long fingers of tall, dried weeds brushed against the bare skin of her legs as she forged a path to the small opening of the cave. She knelt down in front of the cave entrance, which was secured with a heavy door made from thick steel bars. To her, it had always resembled a jail cell for gnomes. She slipped the key into the rusted lock and tried to turn it.

"I think it's too rusted to open." Josephine twisted the key back and forth. "It's not opening."

Logan slipped his backpack off his shoulders, dropped it on the ground, and joined her. He knelt down beside her and studied the lock.

"Careful—if you don't handle it gently, the key will snap in two."

He was close to her—closer than he'd ever been before. His golden-brown skin was hot and sweaty from their hike, and there was something appealing about his natural scent. Her senses were stimulated in a completely unexpected way. She had always liked the way Brice smelled after he had applied cologne, but she couldn't really remember physically responding to the scent of his skin.

"Do you want to give it a try?"

She stood up and stepped back to give him room. Logan, she noticed, was a focused worker. All of his attention was aimed at coaxing the lock open. For a man with such developed arms—truly spectacular arms—he seemed to have a very light touch with his hands.

"Any luck?" she asked.

"We're close." He kept his eyes on the lock.

Then she heard a small click and when Logan smiled at her triumphantly, she knew that he had managed to finagle the lock open.

"Bingo," he said. The key chain was handed to her so Logan could twist the lock free of the gate.

Once the gate was unlocked, he sat down on the ground, braced his feet on the rock face, and used the strength of his arms and the leverage created by his legs to wrench the door open. At first, the steel door wouldn't budge.

"It's frozen, but good." Logan took a short break and used the back of his forearm to wipe the sweat off his forehead.

"Do you want me to help?"

"Maybe." He wrapped his fingers around the bars and repositioned his feet. "Let me give it one more try."

He didn't need a third go at the gate. Logan lowered his head, closed his eyes, and grunted from the force he was exerting to force the gate from its frozen position. The muscles in his arms, the biceps and triceps, hardened and bulged beneath his skin; the veins in his neck popped to the surface and she was about to tell him just to forget it. But then, she heard a loud cracking sound, followed by a long, low creak.

"You did it!" she exclaimed. "That's amazing!"

Logan yanked the door all the way open before he stopped. The look on Josephine's face made him smile. Her face, such a pretty face, was transformed. Her cheeks were flushed and her sweet lips were smiling. The fact that he was able to make her smile the way she was smiling now made him feel like he'd accomplished something pretty major.

"Sorry that was so hard." She saw him flexing his

fingers, undoubtedly to work out the stiffness from gripping the steel bars.

He stood up and brushed the dirt and gravel from his cutoff khaki shorts. "No need to apologize. I consider stuff like that to be fun."

The look of a younger Logan flashed across his face in his excitement. That's how he must have looked when he was a boy.

"If you thought that was fun, you're going to love this next part." Her smile grew. She was starting to feel the excitement, the anticipation, of going down into the cave. Like the chapel, it had been years.

"I'm ready, if you're ready."

After a short discussion, they opted to leave Logan's backpack behind. The opening to the cave became smaller and narrower as it descended quickly into the massive main chamber. Josephine led the way with Logan following behind. At the beginning of the cave, the tunnel was large enough for them to walk crouched over. When it became too tight to stand, they both sat down and used their feet to propel themselves forward.

"It's much tighter than I remember," Josephine said. Her legs were already covered with a fine coating of dust and she knew that the sharp-edged shards of rock had scraped the skin of the backs of her thighs. It would have been wise to wear long pants.

She paused for a moment to switch the flashlight to her left hand, so she could use her right hand to help push her body forward.

"Are you okay?" Logan asked her.

She couldn't turn her head around to look at him. The tunnel had become very narrow and cramped. They were nearly lying on their backs, unable to sit upright, surrounded by walls of sediment and granite. The light from the flashlights was the only light available.

"I'm okay. We're coming up to the slide. It's a really sharp drop, FYI."

The "slide," as her family had dubbed it, was the reason why it was inadvisable to crawl on your hands and knees into the cave. It was a drastic drop that could send a person tumbling headfirst into the jagged boulders down below.

"I'll hang back so we have some leeway between us."

The flashlight she kept on her key chain was small enough to clench between her teeth. With both hands free, Josephine cautiously scooted forward to the entrance of the slide. Her feet pushed loose rocks down the incline and she could hear them rolling and rolling and rolling.

She closed her eyes, for just a minute, and then took a deep, calming breath. This was always the only part of the tunnel that made her nervous. Luckily, the tunnel widened at the opening of the slide and she was able to sit up without hitting her head. Bracing her feet on either side of the tunnel wall, she used her hands to push herself slowly onto the slide. The sharp incline of the tunnel was pulling her body forward, and she had to use the strength of her arms and her legs to slow her descent.

"How're you doing?" she called back to him.

"This is awesome!" he said. "How are you doing?"

"So far, so good—the main chamber is at the end of this section of the tunnel."

"Roger that."

The closer they got to the main chamber, the cooler the temperature felt. It would be at least thirty degrees colder in the main chamber than it was aboveground.

Her bare legs and arms were covered with goose bumps as she negotiated the last section of the tunnel into the cave. Able to stand upright, she stepped off the side, careful of her footing, while Logan finished his climb down the slide.

Some loose rocks, and the light from his flashlight, preceded Logan as he made his final descent into the chamber. Soon he was standing next to her, his body throwing off heat in contrast to the frigid air of the cave.

"This is frickin' unbelievable." He moved the beam of his flashlight to different spots around the cave.

She was already starting to feel uncomfortable in the cold. She should have thought to bring a lightweight jacket, but she wasn't really herself this morning. She crossed one arm over her body so she could still maneuver her flashlight.

"This main chamber is the size of two Olympic swimming pools." Her words echoed back to them from the other side of the cave. "And if you look up there…" She shined a light to a ledge on the cave wall. "That's one of the places that the archaeologists believe the prehistoric Americans made their home."

"Incredible," he said in a reverent voice.

She loved the cave and it always made her feel good to find someone else who shared that love and appreciation. It was awesome, and humbling, to stand in the presence of a place that had been home to ancient Native Americans two thousand years before.

"Is there a way to get to the other side?" he asked.

"There is. But it's too dark to be safe today. If you want, we can ask Tyler to help us set up the right equipment." She added, "And there's another tunnel on the other side that leads to several smaller chambers. Archaeologists found a cache of arrowheads there—I'll have to ask Dad if he still has some of them for you to see."

Even though Logan couldn't cross the cave today, he could at least survey the cave landscape for a future exploration. And Josephine didn't seem to be in a hurry. She perched herself on a small natural rock ledge nearby and seemed content to spend some time shining her flashlight at various spots along the far wall. The floor of the main chamber was packed solid with enormous, jagged boulders that didn't appear to be as dangerous as Logan knew them to be from his rock climbing experience. The boulders were uneven and could be very slippery, and the crevasses between the individual boulders could be deadly. Before he would dare cross to the other side, he would have to figure out a way to bring the proper equipment through the narrow tunnel.

"Shoot," he heard Josephine say. "My battery is dying."

"Do you want to use mine?"

"No. My phone has a flashlight. Thanks, though."

He saw the light on her phone turn on and he heard her make a childlike sound of pleasure when her phone flashlight worked, which meant she was back in business. She stood up and walked to over to a flat, elongated boulder nearby. He wasn't expecting her to walk onto the boulder, but that's what she did.

"Where're you heading?" He worked to keep his question light—she didn't seem like the type of woman who appreciated a man even *sounding* like he was trying to boss her around.

"Over to that spot right there. I can't see the right side of the cave from here."

He wanted to tell her to wait. He wanted to tell her to be careful. But, instead, he only said, "Do you mind if I join you?"

"You're welcome to join me. There's enough room. And you get a 180-degree view of the space."

He shined the light from his flashlight directly in front of his next footstep, and occasionally moved the light ahead to mark out his path. Josephine, quickly and with less caution than he would have liked, walked across the first boulder and then made the small jump onto the next boulder beside it. Once he made it to the second long, flat boulder, Logan made it a point to stand close enough to Josephine to catch her if she lost her balance. The darkness and the enormity of the space threw off his equilibrium. He had to imagine that it was doing the same to her.

He heard her sigh, he imagined from contentment of being back in the cave. And he understood why she wanted to risk venturing out onto these flat boulders. Standing there next to Josephine, surrounded by a sea of boulders, Logan was awestruck by the majesty of this dark, cool, underground world. This was a special moment he was sharing with Josephine, a moment that he didn't believe either of them would soon forget.

"Oh! *No!*"

His reverie was interrupted by Josephine's exclamation. His eyes naturally followed the light of her phone as it slipped out of her fingers and falling toward a deep, black crevice. Before he could react, she lunged for the phone and slipped off the side of the boulder. He heard a cracking sound, the sound of bone hitting granite, and he heard her cry out in pain.

His law enforcement training and rock climbing instincts kicked in. Something had thankfully stopped her from falling all the way down into the crevice. With the light of the flashlight, he could see that her position was temporarily stabilized. Her arms were hugging the top of the boulder near where he was crouching.

"What's hurt?" he asked.

He had seen the pinched, pain-stricken expression on her face when he moved the light past her torso to examine her position in the crevice.

"My knee." He heard the distress in her voice. "I hit it on a rock on the way down."

"Does anything feel broken?"

Her thigh was scraped and bloody; from his angle, he couldn't see her knees or her feet.

"No. I don't think so." She gasped. "But I can't move my foot, Logan. It's stuck under this rock."

That was the last thing he wanted to hear. Getting a limb trapped was always a concern for a rock climber. Once trapped, it could be extremely tricky to free a person's limb. If her foot wasn't broken, he could break it while trying to move the rock. And, after assessing the situation, moving the heavy rock was the only choice. Her right foot was pinned beneath it, and there wasn't any wiggle room.

He made certain her position was still secure before he began to execute his plan to move the rock. He silently cursed his decision to leave his backpack full of supplies behind, and knew that he may be making the trip up the tunnel to retrieve it if his first plan wasn't successful.

Three attempts at budging the rock and Logan knew that he needed more leverage than the strength of his arms and legs alone. He knelt down beside Josephine to deliver the news.

"I need my backpack."

"I know." Her voice had a weak quality that put him on alert for shock.

"I'm going to leave you the flashlight, but I need you to shine the light on my path back to the tunnel. Can you do that?"

Josephine took the flashlight and nodded.

It worked in both of their favors that Josephine had managed to remain calm. How long that calm would last—Logan couldn't be certain.

He used a quick and steady approach to climbing through the tunnel to the surface to get his supplies. He used the same approach to get back to Josephine. He knew he needed to remain calm for her sake, but he wasn't completely confident that he could free her without hurting her. The moment he cleared the tunnel, he called out to her, his voice echoing loudly in the chamber.

"Josephine! Shine the light on the path for me!"

He grabbed the tools he intended to use in an attempt to dislodge the large rock and left his backpack near the tunnel entrance. Sure, steady, cautious steps brought him back to Josephine. Once by her side, he knelt down beside her.

"I need your help, Josephine. Are you still with me?"

In the low light, he saw her nod her head.

"Reach down and feel around the side of the rock. Look for a place where I can thread the rope through."

"I...I think there's a place—but it's too small. I can't even put my finger through past my knuckle."

"That's okay," Logan reassured her. "That's okay. We can work with that."

While she held the flashlight, he started the chore

of digging around the rock. It was a tedious, laborious task and it had to work in a tight space without causing Josephine further harm.

"I think I got it," he said to her.

He grabbed his strong climbing rope and threaded it through the space he had just created.

"Talk to me," he commanded gently. Her breathing sounded shallow.

"I'm okay."

"Hang in there with me just a little bit longer, Jo." Logan quickly wrapped the rope around his waist several times, climbed down between the boulders, and found a spot where he could brace his legs and feet.

"I'm going to count to three, Jo. When you hear me say 'three,' you need to push the rock. Let me know you can hear me."

"I hear you."

Logan wound the rope around his hands and prepared himself to pull. "This may hurt, Jo."

"Just do it!" she yelled at him.

"One. Two. Three!"

It took all of his strength to pull the rock forward. He groaned loudly from exertion and he heard her scream when the rock moved.

"It's off!" The two words he was waiting to hear pinged around the cold cave walls.

"Can you get your foot free?" He didn't release the tension on the rope. They still weren't out of the woods yet.

"No!" she yelled back. "No!"

Her ability to stay calm was deteriorating. He needed to get her out, and he need to get her out now. He needed to make sure that the rock couldn't roll back onto her foot. He closed his eyes, mustered all of his strength, and with a loud battle cry, he pulled on the rope to move the rock farther away from Josephine. Once he was sure the rock wasn't a threat to her, he crawled back onto the boulder and went back to her side.

"My boot won't budge!"

On his stomach, he leaned down and loosened her shoelaces so she could work her foot free. Then he slipped his arms under her armpits and around her chest and hauled her up onto the boulder.

"I can't feel my foot." Josephine reached down to touch her right foot. "I can't feel my *foot*!"

Logan squatted down next to her. "Put your arms around my neck, Jo."

This was a no-nonsense command that she followed without question. Once her arms were around his neck, Logan used his strong thigh muscles to pick her up carefully. With Josephine in his arms, and the flashlight in his hand to light his way, Logan took one cautious step after another until he had brought them both to safety.

Chapter Seven

Josephine held on to Logan's neck as tightly as she could. All of her bravery, all of her stoicism, had evaporated. In their place now were anxiety and pain. Her foot, which she hadn't been able to feel moments ago, was starting to throb. She was starting to notice, for the first time, that her knees hurt and her upper thighs felt raw. She had banged her body up nicely and she was lucky that Logan could remain calm in a crisis.

"I'm going to put you down right here, okay?" he told her.

"Okay." She looked down where he was planning on setting her, straining in the dark to see.

Gently, slowly, he set her down on the cold floor. He opened his backpack to find what he needed. First, he helped her into a lightweight jacket. She had been cold since they entered the main chamber, and had been shivering for a while. The jacket felt like much-needed relief.

"I'm going to wrap your foot over the sock to help protect it, alright?"

He was using a very calm, soothing voice to keep her in the loop. And she found that she liked the sound of his voice—it was quiet, which limited the echo, and confident.

But the minute he touched her foot, her pain level intensified and she jerked her leg back instinctively.

"I'm sorry. I'm sorry," she said, her teeth grit hard together. "I can't do that. It hurts too much."

"I have to wrap it, Jo. If I don't, you're going to be one hurting puppy going through the tunnel."

She had been in such distress that she hadn't given much thought to the trip up the tunnel. Now, after she couldn't have Logan touch her foot, a suffocating feeling of dread swept over her body. How was she going to get back up to the surface? *How?*

Logan must have noticed that her breathing had changed. She was starting to hyperventilate. Her foot was throbbing and felt like someone had smashed it with a meat cleaver. She could not go up that tunnel. She just couldn't do it.

"Jo, what do you do when you need to calm down?"

In a choppy, breathy voice, she said, "Listen—to—music."

"Well, I don't have a radio. But I can sing for you."

"Are—you—any—good?"

Logan's laugh—a deep, rich laugh—sounded good to her ears; Logan's steadying hand on her calf, a warm, strong hand, felt good on her skin.

"Karaoke champion two years in a row."

"That's…impressive."

He laughed again. "Do you have any requests, madam?"

"Surprise—me."

"Okay. I'll sing you one of my favorites," he said. "Now, Jo, when I start wrapping your foot, focus on my voice. Don't think about anything but my voice. Okay? Are you with me?"

"I'm—with you."

And then he started to sing for her. He couldn't have known it, but the song he chose, Bill Withers's "Lean on Me," was one of her favorite songs, too.

He had a million-dollar singing voice. Smooth and deep—it cut through her anxiety and her pain. The acoustics of the cave made it seem that his voice was swirling around her, enveloping her. It wasn't hard to focus on his voice, because it was everywhere. And it was beautiful.

"Ow!" Her concentration broke when he started to wrap her instep. "That's too tight. It's too tight!"

"It has to be this tight." He insisted. "You're doing great, Jo. Almost done."

Her breathing was already steadier and even though the throbbing from her swollen foot was creeping up her leg, she didn't feel as panicked. She just needed to brace herself against the pain.

Logan continued with his song before he continued wrapping her foot. She squeezed her eyes shut and forced herself to focus on his voice.

She smiled right before she grimaced when Logan wrapped the bandage around the ball of her foot. And then she smiled again, in relief, when he announced that he was done.

"How's that feel?"

"Better." The compression helped the throbbing and his singing had helped her calm down. She had managed to get a hold of herself, which could only make things easier for the both of them.

"You're going to have to crawl out on your hands and knees, Jo. It's the only way. I'm going to follow up the rear, so you're not alone in this. I'll catch you if you fall."

Logan bandaged her knees, put on his backpack, and then lifted her into the tunnel. She had already determined that she wasn't going to complain or cry or even so much as make one whimper. She was going to be tough and strong and stoic. She had already "lost it" in front of Logan—she refused to let it happen again.

Slowly, painfully, she crawled upward on her hands and knees. She tried, but she couldn't always keep her injured foot elevated. Whenever she accidentally let it drop and it came in contact with the unforgiving surface of the tunnel floor, she had to clamp down on her lip to stop herself from crying out. At those times, she had to stop. She had to take a break and regroup. Logan stayed close, but not too close. He was encouraging and supportive without rushing her. She appreciated that. She *needed* that. At one point, he told her that he needed to take a break. She knew that the break was for her. He had her lie down on her side to take pressure off her knees and hands. When she was ready, she started again. Together, inch by inch, foot by foot, they climbed to the surface. It wasn't until the warm, late-morning sun touched her face and she smelled the pine in the air that she felt like she was out of danger.

Just outside of the cave entrance, she collapsed onto her back, arm over her arms, and tried to catch her breath. Jagged rocks dug into her back, but she didn't care.

"Lie still for a moment," Logan said.

"No problem." She kept her eyes closed—they needed time to adjust from the dark of the cave to the light of the day.

He was respectful during his examination, always letting her know where and when he was going to touch her. She was dirty and grimy, and she could detect the pungent scent of stress sweat overtaking the barrier of her clinical-strength deodorant. Under normal circumstances, she would have been horrified to have a man, other than Brice, touch her while she was in this condition. But Logan was a professional. He was a cop and trained to handle emergencies. The only thing she felt right now was relieved that he was here to help her.

"I'm not finding any other obvious injuries." Logan sat back on his heels. "That's the good news."

Josephine opened her eyes and blinked several times rapidly until her eyes adjusted to the sunlight. "And the bad news?"

"Your phone is in the cave and I left mine back at the ranch." He pulled a bottle of water from his sack. "I'm going to have to carry you out of here.

"Let's sit you up." Logan held out his arm, clasped her elbow with his hand, and eased her gently into the seated position.

Josephine took a couple of small sips of the water. She already felt like she needed to relieve her bladder. She handed the bottle back to him.

"Can you do that?" she asked him. With all of that muscle, he outweighed her for sure. But they were nearly the same height. How was he going to carry her all the way back to the ranch? It seemed like an unlikely plan.

He gave her a sharp look. "I can do it."

"I just meant—maybe I could stay here while you go get help."

"Negative." He stuffed the water bottle back into the pack and zipped it close. "I'm not leaving you behind."

His attention returned to her. "When I start carrying you, it's going to put a lot of pressure on you. It's going to be a bumpy ride. If you think you need to relieve yourself, let's do it now."

Blunt, to the point. She wasn't used to that approach. But she could respect it. He was focused on getting her home safely. And her bladder did feel full and she imagined that the jostling was only going to make that worse.

"Yes." She nodded. "Thank you."

Logan picked her up in his arms and carried her to a spot, not too far away, but completely private for her to take care of business. When she was finished, he caught her hopping on one foot and was by her side. Once he had her situated on a flat boulder nearby, he disappeared into the woods for a moment himself. He returned quickly, split the last of the water with her, and then left his backpack near the entrance of the cave. Before he returned to her side, he closed the door to the cave and relocked it.

Josephine watched him silently. She had caused all of this mess because she had strayed away from the security of the walls of the cave. If she had been more cautious, they wouldn't be in this situation.

"I'm sorry about all of this," she thought to say.

"I don't want you to worry about that right now." He dried his palms off on his shorts. "We've got another challenge we need to manage together. Let's focus on that."

Logan helped her stand and then knelt down, his back

facing her. He instructed her to climb aboard, yet she hesitated. Because she was tall, she was heavier than she looked. Yes, he outweighed her—but, by how much?

"Josephine." Firm and commanding, that was the tone he used. "I'm going to get you out of here, but I need you to cooperate. You've got to trust me."

Josephine knew she had to relinquish control. It was difficult, but it had to be done. As he had directed, she climbed onto his back and wrapped her arms around his neck. He hooked his arms beneath her thighs and then told her to "hold on and stay straight" while he stood up. He had thickly muscled thighs, but she was still surprised when he was able to stand with the weight of her body on his back.

"We're movin' out, Jo. Are you ready?" he asked.

She hadn't ridden on someone's back since she was a teenager. Back then, it had only been for a short distance and had been fun. This piggyback ride, on the other hand, wasn't any fun at all. Besides the expected pain from her injured foot and her scraped-up knees, her arms felt like they were being wrenched from her arm sockets and her shoulder muscles had started to burn soon after Logan started walking. It also seemed like they had to stop frequently so he could reposition her on his back. She had unintentionally choked him a couple of times, and because she wanted to watch where they were going, he had to remind her time and again, not to lean to one side or the other and throw them off balance.

"Need another break?" Logan's question broke the silence.

"Yes." The word was pushed out of her body as he shifted her into a more secure position.

They found a spot to rest near the stream. Logan took

a folded, clean handkerchief out of his pocket and saturated it with the cold stream water. He brought if over to Josephine for her to cool off her face and neck.

"Thank you." She handed it back to him after she wiped off her face, neck, and the front of her chest.

While he rinsed the handkerchief in the stream for his use, she rubbed her sore shoulders.

"We've made some good progress." He stood in front of her, wiping the sweat off of his face and arms and chest, seemingly unaffected by the fact that he had just carried her for nearly half a mile. He was a little winded, and there was a flushed undertone to the tanned skin of his face, but other than that, carrying her didn't appear to have sapped much of his strength.

A couple more minutes and Logan insisted that they hit the trail once again. He was concerned about the swelling that had traveled past her ankle and into her calf. In silence, they traveled, along the shaded path that wound down the mountain. Exhausted, Josephine turned her head to the side and rested it on Logan's shoulder. She closed her eyes, and tried, *tried*, to ignore all of the places on her body that hurt while Logan pressed on. He was a determined, goal-oriented man—this much she had discovered about him. He was taking her safe return back to the ranch very personally.

"Hey!" Logan yelled.

Josephine's eyes snapped open. She lifted up her head and saw what had caught Logan's attention. Through the trees, she spotted a truck driving across the small pasture at the bottom of the mountain.

"Hold on to me tight, Jo!" Logan's big voice boomed in her ear. "I'm going to try to catch them!"

She clamped her thighs harder around his waist and

forced herself to find a reserve of strength in her arms to hold on without strangling him. Logan leaned forward just a little bit more and started to half jog, half shuffle down the gradual incline to the bottom of the mountain. Once they cleared the tree line, they both screamed at the truck. Logan's breathing was labored now and her arms were wet with the sweat that was pouring off his face and neck. He didn't give up. She felt his legs give way, but he caught them and kept moving forward. He didn't stop until he heard her say to him excitedly, "They saw us!"

Logan stumbled again and he landed on his knees. "I've got to put you down. I'm sorry. I've got to put you down."

She rolled off his back and landed in the grass. Logan was kneeling beside her, head back, eyes closed as if he were in pain. He was breathing like he'd just run a marathon, his face was bright red, and his entire torso was drenched in sweat.

It was instinctive for her to reach out and touch his hand. "Are you okay?"

"Leg cramped up on me," he finally said. Then he opened his eyes to look at her. "I dropped you. I'm sorry."

"Please don't…" Her words were cut off by the sound of the truck door slamming and the sound of her brother's voice calling her name.

"Jo!" Tyler ran to her side. "What happened?"

"I slipped in the cave." Josephine explained in a rush. "Logan saved me."

There was a silent moment of gratitude that passed from her brother to Logan.

"She needs to have that foot x-rayed." Logan nodded to her bandaged foot.

Tyler nodded his understanding as he picked her up

and carried her to the truck. Clint, one of the workers on the ranch, had dropped the bed of the truck down.

"Clint, grab that blanket, man. It's scorchin' back here."

Clint ran to the front of the truck, grabbed the blanket, and then fumbled his way through unfolding it. Once the blanket was in place, Tyler set her down on it. Tyler climbed in the back of the truck with her, while Clint got behind the wheel.

"Hop in, buddy!" Tyler waved his hand at Logan.

Logan was standing now, hands on his hips, still a little winded from the exertion he had used to bring her to safety.

"You go on and get Jo some help." He shook his head. "I left my pack back at the cave. I'm gonna go get it."

Tyler nodded and knocked on the glass so Clint would know that they were ready to head back to the ranch. Clint drove in a semicircle onto the road. For a moment, Josephine couldn't see Logan. She twisted her head around. It was inexplicable—she didn't like the idea of losing sight of him. When was able to see him again, she experienced the oddest sense of relief.

Their eyes met, as if for the first time. The man, who had carried her down the mountain, stood on the road, his hands resting on his hips. Strong, sweaty, and sexier than any man she had ever seen. No words passed between them, but it seemed like the air was filled with silent words. Never taking his eyes off her, Logan trailed behind the slow moving truck with a noticeable limp. When he stopped moving, he lifted his hand up and waved it one single time. She waved back and continued to stare after him until the truck rounded the corner and he disappeared from view.

* * *

Later that evening, Josephine was stretched out on the couch in "wedding central" with her foot elevated. It was a severe sprain, not a fracture, which was a relief. She wouldn't have to hobble down the church aisle with a cast on her foot. It wasn't the best outcome, but it certainly wasn't the worst either. Much worse could have happened to her if it weren't for Logan's quick thinking.

Logan.

He had been on her mind. She had hoped to see him at the dinner table, but he didn't join the family for dinner. Tyler mentioned that he had returned to the cabin, so at least she knew that he had returned from the mountain safely.

"Your brother told me that it's not fractured. That's good news, right?"

Josephine looked up from the pile of RSVPs she was cataloging. She had been so completely focused in her own world, and perhaps a bit foggy from the Tylenol 3, that she didn't hear his footsteps on the hardwood floors.

She put down the RSVP on her lap and smiled at him. "Hey. We missed you at dinner."

"I was beat." Logan was still standing in the doorway. "I fell asleep and just woke up a while ago."

"I bet." She nodded. "Do you want to sit down?"

"I don't want to wear you out," he said.

"You won't." She wanted him to stay. "I need company."

Logan sat down on the ottoman that was just across from the couch. She could tell that he was fresh out of the shower—the air had the clean, crisp scent of soap and shampoo.

She smiled at him affectionately. "I really need to thank you for what you did for me today."

He leaned forward, forearms resting on his thighs, hands clasped together. "You don't need to thank me. I was just doing my job."

He had such a nice mouth.

"I know," she said. "But, I still need to thank you. So—thank you."

"You're welcome." He smiled briefly with a slight nod. "Did you have a chance to talk to Brice?"

Josephine felt her chest tighten when Logan mentioned Brice's name. She still felt sick to her stomach when she heard it, and he was the last person she wanted to talk about.

"Why do you ask?" She tried, very hard, to keep her voice as normal as possible.

He was a cop, so he was trained to notice small details. There was a slight shift in his dark brown eyes— she was sure certain he had detected something odd in her voice and her question.

He responded. "You were out hiking alone with a guy he doesn't know. Some people still don't believe that men and women can be friends."

"Oh." She had a frown etched into her brow that she couldn't control. "Well, you don't have to worry about that. Brice and I aren't together anymore."

It took him a second to process her statement. He had been worried, for Josephine's sake, about Brice's reaction. He had also been worried that a bad reaction from Brice would taint his budding friendship with Josephine.

There was a moment when he looked directly into her bright, aqua-blue eyes and she didn't look away. And that's when he read the hurt in her eyes that wasn't a result of her sprained ankle—it was a direct result of her broken heart.

"I'm sorry to hear that..." he finally said. It was the standard answer that was given in a situation like this and his delivery had sounded sincere. But, was it true? Was he really *sorry to hear* that Brice had done a truly stupid thing by letting Josephine Brand slip through his fingers?

No. He wasn't. Not one bit.

Chapter Eight

That first visit rolled into the next, and soon Logan was coming to check on her every afternoon after he had finished working on the relocation of the chapel. She had begun to count on those visits. She had begun to look forward to them. In fact, she had started to look at the clock, anticipating his arrival. And if he was late, she felt disappointed. Yes, she had plenty of things to keep her busy while she let her foot heal—she was getting a ton of schoolwork done and she loved immersing herself in the wedding with her mom and Jordan. But, her daily visit from Logan was what she looked forward to the most.

"Jo." Her sister's voice interrupted her internal dialogue. *"Jo!"*

Josephine shifted her eyes from the window to her sister, who was now standing in front of her wearing her wedding dress.

"Oh, Jordy—it's beyond." She set her laptop off to the side and swung her legs off the couch.

Her sister had chosen an Eve of Milady wedding gown from the couture line. The sweetheart bodice was hand-beaded and the fit-and-flare long skirt was made of fine silk organza. There was an edge to the gown, with its completely sheer back, that matched Jordan's personality perfectly.

She stood up. She need to get a closer look at the gown she had helped her sister select. When she eventually married, she wanted to wear a ball gown. But this sleek, sophisticated silhouette was her twin to a tee.

Her foot felt like it was almost healed when she walked the couple of steps over to where Jordan was standing.

"Have you seen yourself?" she asked her sister.

Jordan nodded. "Would you zip the back for me?"

Josephine raised the zipper carefully. "Where's Mom? She should be here for this."

She was about to call out for their mom, but Jordan stopped her.

"I want it to be just the two of us for a minute. Then we'll call Mom. Okay?"

"Okay," Josephine said with a question in her tone.

Her sister turned around to face her and they naturally reached for each other's hands. Quietly, Josephine admired her twin and the beauty of the dress.

"You are so stunning in this gown, Jordy—you take my breath away."

"Thanks, sis." Jordy hugged her before she asked, "Are you okay, though? I mean, *really* okay?"

Josephine glanced down at her ankle and moved it around. "I'm almost back to 100 percent."

"I didn't mean that. I meant, are you okay with the wedding? With what happened with Brice."

Whenever Brice's name came up, her stomach muscles tightened unpleasantly. Why did everyone insist on talking about him? When she was dating him, no one wanted to talk about him. Now that they were broken up—she couldn't get them to *stop*!

Josephine took a step back and said with a stiff smile. "Let's not ruin a perfectly wonderful moment by bringing up the *B* word. Okay?"

Ever since they were little girls, they could feel each other's pain. Josephine knew that Jordan could feel her pain now. The forced smile didn't fool her.

"You're right. I shouldn't've brought up the jerk. My bad. I'm just worried…the wedding is making you sad."

"*Sad?* What are you talking about? You know I love weddings. If anything, helping you and Mom with all of the planning has kept my mind occupied."

"No. I know you love weddings, Jo. It's just that both of us always thought that you'd get married first…"

"Well, that's how it turned out and that's okay." Josephine met her sister's eyes and held them to make certain Jordan understood that she was sincere. "Yes, I've been feeling a little sad. But, it doesn't have anything to do with your wedding. *That* only makes me feel happy."

Her sister's reply was waylaid by the sound of grinding gears and squealing brakes. Josephine and her sister's attention turned to the commotion outside.

"Looks like they're pouring the foundation today." Jordan moved closer to the window.

Josephine joined her. Her eyes searched the site up on the hill where the new chapel foundation was being poured; when she found Logan, her search was over.

He had just jumped down from the cab of a large earth mover. It was easy to distinguish him from the other men. The size of the muscles of his bare arms and shoulders, the blackness of his hair—he stood out.

"Don't you just love a man with big equipment?" her sister asked her.

She could feel Jordan staring at her knowingly—she had been caught staring at Logan. There was no sense trying to deny it.

"Brice who, right?" Jordan asked, rhetorically.

"Quit bringing up Brice! I don't want to talk about him."

"An honest mistake," Jordan confessed. "Let's go show Mom my dress."

"Sounds like a plan. Let me grab this box of tissues. You know that waterworks are going to flow the minute Mom sees you."

After dinner, Josephine walked, for the first time without crutches, out to the campfire. She passed Jordan, Ian, and Shadow on their way to the guesthouse. When she reached the edge of the fire, Tyler stood up and handed Logan his guitar.

"Where are you going?" she asked her brother.

"Hittin' the hay." Tyler adjusted his hat on his head. "I'm plumb wore out, sissy."

Her father flicked the stub of his cigar into the fire and stood up. "I suppose it's time for me to hit the hay, too."

"What? I show up and everyone clears out?" Josephine said, half teasing, half serious, as she hugged her father good-night.

She called after Hank. "I can smell the smoke on your shirt, Dad!"

She heard her father laugh before he called back to her, "It'll clear off before I get back to the house."

Josephine looked after her father and brother for a minute and then, arms crossed over her chest, she asked Logan in a playfully stern tone, "I suppose you're going in now, too?"

Logan looked up from the task of tuning her brother's old guitar. "Not me. I made the mistake of having two cups of coffee at dinner, so…sleep's going to be a long time comin'." He nodded to the seat next to him. "Keep me company."

Josephine didn't have to think about whether or not she wanted to join him. She did. Logan had an easygoing nature that she appreciated. It was in stark contrast to her personality, and it was certainly in contrast to Brice's conservative, rigid, type-A personality. She tried not to compare them, but found it almost impossible *not to* compare them. And, even though Brice's personality was so close to hers, and she was attracted to his serious, always-on-task persona, Logan's laid-back, devil-may-care attitude was a refreshing change. Was it a change that she wanted for the long term? She wasn't sure about that. Brice had always been the plan in her head and it was hard to imagine walking through life with another man—especially a man who was so different than Brice. But, for now, it felt…comfortable… to be with Logan.

Josephine grabbed a nearby stick and poked the logs in the fire pit to stoke the small flames. She was wearing a long-sleeved top made of thin cotton, and wished now that she had grabbed her lightweight jacket before she headed out of the house. But, she had been in a rush to get down to the campfire. She had been cooped up in the house healing her ankle all week and she felt a little stir-crazy. And, if she were honest to herself, she wanted to see Logan. He hadn't stopped by to see her, as was usual, and he wasn't at dinner. Her brother mentioned that Logan was video chatting with his uncle, making the final arrangements for relocating the chapel.

"Here, you look cold." Logan leaned toward her, his arm extended, holding out a rolled flannel shirt.

"Don't you need it?" She took the shirt gratefully.

"Nah, I'm good." He strummed lightly on the guitar strings. "Got any requests?"

She slipped her arms into the shirt and pulled it tightly in front of her, then crossed her arms once again. She rocked back and forth a little while she thought.

"Surprise me," she finally said.

"You like James Taylor?"

Surprised, she smiled at him. "Love him."

"Me, too…"

Tucked warmly inside of his shirt, a shirt that looked like it had seen a lot of years and use, Logan began to play her favorite James Taylor song, "Fire and Rain." She had heard his singing voice when he sang to her in the cave to keep her calm. He had a beautiful voice— the kind of voice that made a woman stop and listen. The kind of voice that sent chills popping up all over her body.

In the firelight, Josephine watched Logan as he played the guitar and sang. He was giving her a private concert, and the moment was—special. Intimate. It was the perfect setting, and the perfect moment, for lovers.

Even though they weren't lovers, there was a connection there. She felt it, and she could tell that Logan felt it too.

She had always found him to be handsome, ever since the first day. It was undeniable. The dark hair, tanned skin, eyes the color of aged brandy. Not to mention his incredibly fit body. But when she first met him, she had been Brice's girl. His handsomeness hadn't mattered.

She wasn't Brice's girl anymore, was she? And Logan's handsomeness had become much more interesting to her lately.

At the end of the song, Logan looked over at Josephine. Her eyes were closed and the light from the fire was casting a beautiful array of yellow and gold across the delicate features of her face. Halfway through the song, she had started to sing with him. And their voices were a perfect complement. There had been only one other woman whose voice had complemented his voice, with whom he loved to sing duets, but he could hardly remember what it felt like to sing with her. This moment—this night—was all about lovely, sweet Josephine.

"You have a really good voice. I didn't know you sang." He smiled at her.

Josephine's aqua-blue eyes opened wide, in surprise. "I didn't realize I was singing out loud."

He could feel her embarrassment, as much as he could see it. "You should sing out loud all the time."

"Only in the shower."

"That's too bad. You've got a great voice."

She smiled at him, almost shyly. "I was a choir geek all through high school."

Logan stroked the strings, one by one, with his thumb. "I tried to date all the choir geeks in high school."

"Oh, yeah?" She leaned forward and rested her elbows on her legs. "Any luck?"

"Some." His answer was casual, but Josephine detected a deeper undercurrent beneath that one, simple word. "Give me another song—one that you like to sing. I might know it," he said.

"Um, let me think. You wouldn't happen to know any Judds' songs, would you?"

Logan played a couple of chords. "Do you know the lyrics to this one?"

"'Why Not Me,'" she said. Logan had an uncanny ability to pick her favorite songs. Brice hated country music, so she had stopped listening to it when he was around to be courteous. What was strange, and she hadn't really thought about it until just now, but she had stopped singing when Brice was around several years ago.

"You sing. I'll play."

"No way, Jose! If I sing, you sing."

"Alright," he agreed. "Do you want to be Mamma Judd or Wynonna?"

"Wynonna."

"I was afraid you were going to say that." Logan shook his head with a small smile.

Beneath the large expanse of the blue-black starless sky, they sang their first song together. She hadn't sung a duet since high school, and singing with Logan was as natural as walking or talking. They just fit. They were able to pick harmony together and anticipate what the other would do next. In singing, at least, they were a compatible pair.

By the end of the song, Josephine was laughing. She

wasn't laughing because anything was funny—but because singing again had made her feel good inside.

"You're really good, Josephine." Logan rested his arm on the top of the guitar, which was resting on his thigh.

"No, you're good." Josephine beamed at him. "Who taught you to sing like that?"

"My mom, mainly—and singing in church." He slipped the guitar pick between two strings. "How 'bout you?"

"The same. You should hear my mom sing. She's really got some amazing pipes."

Logan stood up, stretched, and then held out his hand to her. "So do you."

She didn't argue with him—instead, she took his offered hand and stood up as well.

"Looks like your ankle's healing nicely," he said, looking down at her foot.

"Can't complain." She held out her foot a little. "Now, if only my replacement phone would get here, everything'll be copacetic. What a stupid move that was—my whole life was on that phone."

He walked beside her, keeping pace with her slow pace as they headed back toward the ranch house.

"Maybe you needed a break," he suggested quietly. "Maybe you needed to start over."

"Maybe," she agreed thoughtfully. "Maybe."

When her replacement phone arrived, she couldn't wait to get it out of the box. It had felt like she had been missing a vital appendage without her constant phone companion. However, once it was out of the box and she had it set up just like her "lost forever to the cave" phone, she had a serious lapse in judgment and checked social media.

She had actually thought that she was doing fine— that she was handling the sudden "dumping" from her first love pretty well. Yes, there had been a couple of nights that she had cried herself to sleep in the fetal position, but she wasn't thinking about Brice every minute of every day and she hadn't allowed herself to dwell on trying to create a mental picture in her head of the woman who had captivated him.

Once she checked social media, she was reminded again what the other woman looked like. Brice had put posted several pictures of himself, *at his parents' estate*, with a knock-out brunette with a Sofía Vergara–type body. All Josephine could do, for several long, painful seconds was to stare at the new woman in Brice's life. Brains, beauty, and a bangin' body—no wonder he'd defected.

Josephine slammed the phone facedown on her comforter and flopped back onto the pillows. She couldn't *un-see* those pictures—she only wished that she could. Her hand moved to her chest. Brice had always told her that he didn't mind her size A cups. He'd given her the "brains over boobs" speech on several occasions. And yet, in the end, he'd traded her in for a shiny new floor model that came standard-equipped with brains *and* boobs.

She grabbed her pillow, covered her face, and screamed as loud as she could. Then she did it again. That picture triggered all of the jealousy and disappointment and anger she had suppressed. It was bubbling to the surface like magma pouring out of a volcano.

She wanted to hit something. She wanted to kick

something. In all honesty, she really wanted to punch Brice in his stupid face!

Josephine pushed the pillow off her face and sat upright. She needed to go outside and clear her head. She had intended to study, but now she couldn't. She just *couldn't*.

She swung her long legs off the bed, yanked on her hiking boots, and headed downstairs. Her plan was to race past the kitchen, where her mom was sure to be, and get outside without talking to anyone. She hit the second floor landing and smelled the delicious scent of homemade root beer and sweet-potato pie. Since her daughters had arrived home, her mom had spent at least part of her day happily baking homemade goodies that she knew that they loved.

As she raced past the kitchen entrance, Josephine called to her mom, "I'll be outside if you need me."

Not waiting for her mom's answer, she shot out the door, slammed it behind her harder than she had intended, and then hurried down the porch steps. She needed a place where she could be alone—a place where she could unleash some of this newfound fury without an audience. And she was going to go there right now.

Logan pulled one of Bent Tree's trucks in a spot near the barn and turned off the engine. He noticed Josephine walking quickly toward a small structure that was farther away from the working barns. He didn't know what was in that building—from the looks of it, he'd assumed that it was an old storage barn. Josephine always caught his attention—he was always hoping to catch sight of her. Not only was she easy-on-the-eyes, but he liked her. He *really* liked her. He had started to know her mannerisms—the way she walked, the way she talked, the way her eyes twinkled when she smiled. Today, there was something different about her. Her shoulders were stiff, her hands were balled up, and she was looking down at the ground.

Perhaps it was the wrong thing to do, he acted on gut-instinct alone, but he followed her. He got out of the truck without giving it much thought and went after her. When he was close to the building, he could hear faint sounds drifting through the cracked-open door. It sounded like *grunting*, and he hoped he wasn't about to come upon something that he really didn't want to see.

Logan opened the door wide enough for him to look inside. In the middle of the small building, hanging from the rafters, was an old heavyweight punching bag. The only light that was coming into the building was from the areas of the walls where the wooden planks were missing. Josephine was standing in front of the bag, oblivious that he was watching from the doorway, intent on beating the bag with her small fist.

The expression on her face, in what he assumed to be an unmasked, private moment, could only be described as anguished. Sweat had darkened the hair around her face and long pieces were stuck to the side of her neck as she pounded the bag with the side of her hand. She hit the bag again and again. He thought she would notice him; when she didn't, he started to believe that perhaps it was best that she hadn't.

Logan took a step back from the door, and turned to leave. But when he heard her curse and yell "Ow," he changed his mind.

"You're hitting it wrong." He pushed the door to the building open wider to let the light in.

Winded and sweaty and disheveled, Josephine stared at him. She didn't bother to try to hide the raw pain in her eyes when he got closer to her. And she didn't tell him to leave.

"You're hitting like a girl."

"I *am* a girl."

"No, I meant that if you keep hitting it like that you're going to hurt your hand," he told her.

"Then show me the right way," she snapped.

She didn't apologize for snapping at him, and he didn't expect one. They both knew that he was the one invading her privacy.

"First we need to get your stance solid." Logan adopted a fighting stance, his right foot back, his left foot forward, his knees slightly bent. He waited for Josephine to copy him and then showed her the proper way to punch.

"Ball your fingers up firmly, with your thumb wrapped around your pointer finger—like this..." He instructed. "Now put both of your arms up to protect your face and your chest—like so—your elbows are in to protect your ribs. When you punch..." He demonstrated by showing her how to execute a forward jab. "Your arm comes out straight—at this point, your fingers should be relaxed, and right before your impact of your target, that's when you tighten your fist up."

Logan stepped closer to her, took the spot in front of the bag, and punched the bag hard.

The rusty chain holding up the bag creaked when it swung back toward them. Logan caught the dusty bag to stop it from swinging.

"Now you do it," he told her.

Josephine adopted the fighting stance, balled up her

fist, and held up her arms, just like he had instructed. Then, with a straight arm and solid follow-through, she jabbed the dirty punching bag. To her ears, the bag made a satisfying "thud" sound when she hit it.

"That really felt good." She smiled at Logan with a natural, satisfied smile. "I'm doing that again."

Chapter Nine

For the next hour, Josephine learned how to punch the bag properly. Logan taught her how to jab the bag, slow and steady, without hurting her hand. And then he showed her how to rapid punch using both hands. Once she had the hang of it, Logan stepped behind the bag and held it in place so she could hit the bag as many times as she wanted. He didn't say a word and she was glad he didn't. She wanted to focus on punching the bag, again and again and again.

Every time she hit the bag, she imagined that she was hitting Brice. In her mind, with every strike, she was yelling at him.

You stupid jerk! You pompous ass! I trusted you! I loved you! I wasted five years of my life on you! And you ruined everything!

She hit the bag and hit the bag and hit the bag until

her arms ached and her knuckles were red. When she was too tired to throw one more punch, she sat down on the ground and tried to catch her breath. She was completely spent physically, and she felt better mentally.

Logan joined her. "Feel better?"

Her head was lowered, her knees bent, her arms wrapped around her shins. She nodded "yes."

In silence, they sat on the dirt floor of the abandoned storage shed, while Josephine had a chance to recover. So much of her anger had been spent, but what was left, what remained, was a deep sense of loss. A deep sense of sadness. Brice had been a big part of her life—he had been more than her lover. He had been her confidant, her best friend. They had talked every day and he was the first one she called when something exciting happened to her. But now, all of that was gone. It felt like a death.

She couldn't stop what happened next. She couldn't help what happened next. The tears started to pour out of her eyes, as if they were flowing directly from her heart onto the cheeks of her face. She pressed her forehead hard onto her knees and bear-hugged her legs so tightly that her arm muscles shook from the strain.

Josephine felt Logan move closer, felt him put his arm around her shoulders for support. She didn't pull away, but she couldn't fully accept him, either. She stiffened beneath the weight of his arm and couldn't lean on him. Brice was the one who was supposed to give her comfort and support. Brice was The One. But he was gone. She knew that now. A picture speaks a thousand words, the saying goes, and seeing Brice at his parents' house with Caroline told her more than she wanted to know. He looked happy. Had he ever looked that happy in pictures with her?

"No!" She answered the question in her head out loud with a shake of her bent head.

She sniffed loudly, trying to get some air through her clogged nose. Unable to breathe through her nose at the moment, she took a breath in through her mouth and used her shirt to wipe the tears from her face. She pulled away from Logan, and he dropped his arm right away.

Josephine stood up, and Logan followed. She turned her face away from him, embarrassed.

"You must think I'm a real nut job," she said.

"No," he said, quietly. "I think you're grieving."

His response was intuitive and showed a sensitivity that surprised her. Arms crossed tightly in front of her body, Josephine glanced at him.

Logan saw the question in her eyes. "I've been in your shoes."

"Who did you lose?" she asked.

"My wife."

Josephine looked directly into his eyes—unshuttered eyes that let her glimpse the heart inside of the man.

"Did she die?" It was an inelegant question, but she wanted to know. She hadn't even known that he had been married.

"No," he said. "But it felt like she had."

"What happened?"

Logan didn't turn look away when he said, "I wasn't enough for her. She wanted something else. Someone else."

"I'm sorry," she said, and she meant it. She was sorry for anyone who had felt the same kind of sharp pain she was feeling right now.

"It was a long time ago and I've moved on."

"Well…at least there's a little hope for me yet."

"There's hope—just don't let yourself get stuck."

She knew exactly what he meant. He was telling her not to wallow. Mourn and then move on, because Brice already had.

Logan pushed the door open wider and let her walk through first. The bright sun hurt her eyes, but the heat, which she normally liked, only made her feel hotter and stickier. A shower was the only solution.

On the walk back to the house, she asked, "Where'd you learn to box like that, anyway?"

"When you're the scrawniest, shortest little kid in the neighborhood, you either learn how to fight or you accept getting the crap beat out of you on a weekly basis. I figured I couldn't force myself to grow, but I knew I could learn how to fight. So, I did."

She looked at his profile. It was a strong profile. Not aristocratic, like Brice's profile—it was more rugged, more masculine.

"Did the bullies leave you alone?"

"Yeah, they figured out pretty quick not to mess with me anymore. I was little, but I had heart. That's what my uncle called it anyway. All I knew was that I was tired of getting my block knocked off every week."

They both stopped a few feet away from the porch, away from the kitchen windows. "You'll be okay, then, right?"

"Oh, sure." She tried to sound upbeat. "I feel better already. I'm not going to tell any of my fellow pacifists this, but punching does have its perks."

"You're planning to go with us tonight, aren't you?"

Jordan, Ian, her brother, and Logan were all going into town for some dancing and drinking. She had intended to beg off, but now, after having seen Brice out having a great time with his new love interest, she knew that sitting home moping wasn't the answer. She needed to go out and have some fun.

"I'm going." She stopped a few feet away from the porch, away from the kitchen windows. "How do I look?"

"Like you've been crying." Logan examined her face with a critical eye. He slipped off his sunglasses and gave them to her. "Here—wear these."

Josephine put the sunglasses on and then looked at him. "How about now?"

"Beautiful."

She had already discovered that Logan was an honest man, sometimes to the point of being blunt. So she knew that he meant what he said. And, in that moment, perhaps even more so than any other moment, she needed a little ego boost. Being told by a good-looking cop that she was beautiful qualified as a definite ego boost in her book.

"You're a good friend, Logan."

"I try to be," he said. "So, I'll catch you later, then. I've got to get back to work. We're moving the chapel in one day."

"All you've done is work on your vacation," she noted. "When are you going to relax and have some fun?"

Logan smiled at her, walked backward a couple of steps, and lifted both of his hands to gesture to the ranch and the mountains.

"Are you kidding me?" He laughed. "This *is* my paradise."

After Josephine took a long shower, she lay on her bed with a cold washcloth over her eyes. Her eyes were puffy and they stung. And even after several cold washcloth sessions, her eyes still looked like she'd been cry-ing. Her eyes were too sore to study, and she didn't feel like staying cooped up inside anyway. She wouldn't mind working on the wedding, but she didn't feel like explaining her appearance to her mom, which would only lead to yet another discussion about Brice and her "feelings." Instead, she decided to go for a ride.

"Hey. Where're all the horses?" Josephine looked around the empty stable.

London Davenport, an intern from Montana State University, answered her rhetorical question. "Your brother told me to turn them all out in the north pas-ture. So, that's what I did."

"Well, shoot." Josephine frowned, hands on her hips.

London shoveled a large pile of manure and hay into her cart before she closed the stall door. London loaded her pitchfork onto the cart and moved the cart to the next stall.

"You could always take Easy," the intern suggested.

Josephine grimaced at the thought. Easy Does It was the offspring of her grandfather's donkey Nomad and one of Bent Tree's purebred quarter horses. It was an ac-cidental coupling that produced a mule that completely embodied the phrase "stubborn as a mule." Yet he was beloved by all of them and had become a Bent Tree mascot of sorts.

The mule seemed to recognize that they were talk-ing about him, that they were suggesting that he partic-ipate in some sort of undesirable physical exertion, and he turned around so his narrow butt was facing them. It was all the challenge that Josephine needed. She had a rather unfortunate history with this mule, and even though he had outsmarted her before, she was certain that today redemption was within her grasp.

"He looks like he could use some fresh air," she said to London.

London looked at her like she was crazy, and she probably was. "That mule is so barn sour and stuffed full of hay that it's gonna take the two of us to get him out of that stall, you know."

"Are you up for it?"

London was a tall, Nordic-looking blonde who was one of the few women she'd ever met who was taller than she was. The intern had a ranch-wide reputation for being as strong, and as determined, as most of the men.

London gave her a nod. "Just give me a shout when you're ready."

Josephine groomed, saddled, and bridled the mule. And then, she couldn't get the mule out of the stall.

"Need help?" London came up behind her.

"I was hoping that I could convince him to follow me, seeing as we're old friends and all." Josephine frowned at the mule that refused to cross the threshold of the stall into the aisle. "But no such luck."

The intern held up a feed bucket. "This is the only way to get Easy out of the stall nowadays."

With a lot of patience and coaxing and sweet feed, Easy Does It finally put one hoof over the threshold.

"It's going to be dark by the time I get him out of the stall!" Josephine complained.

"He's counting on the fact that you're going to give up." London laughed as she shook the feed bucket just out of the reach of the mule's searching lips.

"Not a chance," Josephine vowed. "I'm going to win this round."

And she did. With London's help, they managed to convince Easy to walk, at a painstakingly slow pace, out of the stall and out of the stable. Josephine easily mounted the short-statured mule and then she squeezed her legs around Easy's hay-filled belly to signal that he should move forward. But he didn't budge.

"Darn it, Easy! Go!" She wiggled a little back and forth to encourage the mule to take one step forward.

She sat on the mule's back, in the same spot, not moving, for a good five minutes before London had mercy on her and came out of the stable carrying the trusty feed bucket. London got Easy moving, and then once he was moving forward, Josephine was able to keep the momentum going.

"Thank you, London!" she called over her shoulder. "Come on, Easy! You can do it!"

She decided to take the road that would eventually take her in the direction of the chapel. Once they made it through the gate, and Easy caught a glimpse of the field ahead, he started to jog. Easy's trot was a choppy, bone-jarring gait that was impossible to ride comfortably. She couldn't sit in the saddle for it, and she had to post at double pace—up, down, up, down, up, down, up!

Easy wasn't easy to get started, but as was fitting with his contrary personality, he was also hard to stop. His jog turned into a canter.

"Whoa! Easy does it, Easy!" She tightened the reins to slow him down.

Easy ignored her command and took off across the field. Josephine grabbed a chunk of his wiry mane, held on, and decided to let him run it out. This was how Easy Does It got his name after all—when her brother first tried to ride him, the entire family could hear him screaming, "Hey! Easy does it, mule! Easy does it!" at the mule when it bolted across the field.

Across the field, Easy's short legs churned until he was tired and then he halted out of the blue. Holding on to the mane stopped her from being catapulted over his head and onto the ground.

"Really, Easy?" She exclaimed loudly. "Really?"

It was a good thing that he had stopped. But getting him started again proved to be a chore. She had imagined herself galloping across the open fields of the ranch, the wind on her face and blowing through her hair. She had imagined a movie scene kind of moment. Instead, she got a Comedy Central kind of moment. She was stuck, in a field, astride an obese, spoiled mascot mule, hot *and* thirsty. She had forgotten to put on bug spray, so there were random bugs buzzing around her, harassing her, harassing Easy, and on top of everything, she seriously needed to pee after suffering the mule's torturous trot.

Josephine moved her hips back and forth. "Move, Easy! Come *on*! Move!"

But she knew he wasn't going to move. In fact, she knew that Easy could stand there for the rest of the day, not moving a muscle. He'd had his run and now he was done. He wasn't about to go one more step in the direction that was taking him away from his stall.

"Fine!" Josephine gave up and gave in. "Easy Does It, two. Josephine Brand, *zero*!"

She turned the mule to the left and Easy headed back to the barn with an animated, brisk walk. The longer she sat in the saddle, the more pain she was starting to feel in her bladder. There was no way she was making it back to the barn without making a pit stop first.

When she asked Easy to stop, and he *did*, she was pleasantly surprised. She tied his reins to a nearby tree and carefully stepped into the brush. She hadn't finished relieving herself when she heard the horrible sound of hooves pounding on dirt.

"Darn it, Easy! Don't you *dare*!" She yanked up her pants halfway and hopped over the brush onto the road.

The mule had managed to untie the reins and was running like a Kentucky Thoroughbred back to the barn. Josephine watched the mule's hind end get smaller and smaller, until he completely disappeared.

"This day sucks!" She threw up her hands. "This day *seriously* sucks!"

She couldn't believe that the mule had managed to leave her stranded *twice* in one lifetime. She quickly zipped up her pants and began the long schlep back to the ranch. Frustrated, annoyed, angry—more emotions sprang up unbidden. Tears, coming from a place of exasperation rather than sadness, ran down her cheeks while she marched forward.

At the halfway mark, Josephine heard the sound of a vehicle coming up the road behind her. She wiped the residual tears from her face onto her T-shirt, and then turned around to see who it was.

"Really?" She looked up at the sky.

It was Logan. How many times did he need to see her at her worst in one day?

"Need a ride?" Logan stopped the truck next to her.

"Yes," she said bitterly. "My mule left me stranded."

"What?" Logan laughed.

She hopped in next to him and slammed the door shut. "That stupid mule, Easy! He managed to untie the reins and then he just took off!"

Logan was still laughing as he shifted into Drive and pressed on the gas. "Why were you riding a mule in the first place?"

"Because Tyler told the intern to turn out all of the horses in north pasture—it was the mule or nothing. I chose the mule." Her social mask had slipped and she couldn't manage pleasantness at the moment.

"You're not having the best day, are you?"

"No." Josephine smashed a mosquito that had dared to land on the truck's dash. "I'm not."

"Well—at least you have tonight to look forward to. You'll dance, you'll drink a little…" Logan told her. "It'll be like today never happened…"

"I'm not going." She stared out the window. Her ability to "rally" and "press on" had vanished along with her mule.

"Oh, come on. You don't want to sit at home and mope…"

"Yes, I do."

He ignored her comment and continued. "I was counting on you to teach me how to do the two-step. I'm a pretty liberal guy, but I'm not going to ask Tyler to teach me."

She turned her head to look at him. "You really want to learn how to line dance? Why?"

"I want the complete cowboy experience while I'm here." Logan smiled at her. "So you've got to come out with us and show me how to dance like a real cowboy. Fair's fair…" He added. "I taught you how to punch, so you should teach me how to dance. One good turn deserves another, don't you think?"

Logan pulled the truck into an empty space in front of the barn and shifted into Park. Through the windshield, Josephine could see Easy was in the paddock attached to his stall and he was munching on a pad of hay. She had sent a text to London to let her know not to send search and rescue out, that she was "okay" and that Easy was heading her way. London offered to come pick her up, but she hadn't wanted the intern to see her crying. But Logan had already seen her cry—so she had taken the ride.

"Jo, what do you think?" Logan asked her.

"Why do you call me 'Jo'?" Hand on the door, Josephine told him, "Only my closest friends and family call me that."

"I don't know. Just seemed natural, I suppose." Logan stopped smiling. "Do you want me to stop?"

"No…" She shook her head. "I was just thinking out loud, really."

Josephine got out of the truck and shut the door behind her. Logan quickly followed her lead, got out, and met her at the back of the truck.

"Thanks for the ride, Logan," she said, walking toward the house. "I'll see you later."

Logan stopped walking, sensing that she needed to be alone. "As in, see you later tonight?"

She nodded. "I'll come. I wouldn't wish line dancing with my brother on my worst enemy, much less a friend."

Logan watched Josephine walk slowly to the house, her long, golden-brown ponytail swaying from one side to the other. He had been attracted to her physically from the beginning when he had pulled her over for speeding. Now that he had gotten to know her, as a woman, as a friend, he knew that there was much more to Josephine than just her pretty face. She was a kind woman— a generous woman, intelligent, humorous. Loyal. Yes, she was a little uptight and structured, but when it came to Josephine, those qualities were endearing to him. He wanted Brice's loss to be his gain. And he didn't know how he was going to manage it, but he fully intended to get the heck out of the "friend zone" ASAP.

Chapter Ten

"Hi, sweetheart. Don't you look nice," her mom said to her when she stepped out onto the porch.

Even though they didn't get to see each other much during the day, it was a ritual for her parents to sit on the porch swing together after dinner. They had the kind of marriage that Josephine had always wanted for herself. Her father adored her mother, and her mother adored him right back. After more than forty years of marriage and raising five children, they still hugged and kissed and laughed together.

"Why don't the two of you come with?" Josephine gave her father a hug.

"No..." Her mother smiled with a shake of her head. "I'm going to spend a quiet night alone with your father for a change."

"Honey, I don't know how quiet of a night it's going

to be…looks like one of the mares is about to give birth," Hank said. "Tyler'll be staying behind tonight either way."

Josephine nodded her understanding. That's how life had always been on the ranch—plans were always tentative because the health of the animals came first.

"Good evening."

Josephine turned toward the sound of Logan's familiar voice. This time, when she heard his voice, something different happened—she felt a nervous excitement in the pit of her stomach.

"Evening, son." Hank smiled easily at Logan. "How are we set for tomorrow?"

It was still hard for her to adjust to Hank referring to Logan as "son." He hadn't started to refer to Ian with that title and he certainly never came close with Brice. But, whether she thought it was appropriate or not, she could see the respect in her father's clear, deeply set blue eyes whenever he interacted with the San Diego cop.

"We're set, sir." Logan rested his arms on the porch railing. "As long as it doesn't rain, we're bringing her down the mountain tomorrow."

Her father looked satisfied and her mother looked irritated. Barbara was displeased with her husband's decision to start such a major project with the June wedding on the horizon. Hank wouldn't be dissuaded. He was determined, as a wedding gift to Jordan, for the chapel to be relocated and presentable for wedding pictures. Her mom was used to getting her way with her father, but not this time.

Logan made it a point to chat with Josephine's parents. Yes, he liked them, but he also knew how close she was with her parents and he wanted her to see that they accepted him. It could only work in his favor.

"Well, we better get going. Are you ready?" he asked Josephine.

He had always thought she was a beauty, from first sight. Yet, tonight, unbelievably, she looked even more radiant to his eyes. She wore her golden-brown hair long and loose, and the little touches of makeup she had applied enhanced the brightness of her turquoise-blue eyes, the highness of her cheekbones, and the fullness of her lips. He had to remind himself not to stare at her face.

Josephine nodded and met him at the bottom of the porch stairs.

"You're dressed like a bona fide cowboy." She gave him a quick once-over.

He glanced down at his getup. The yoked cotton shirt and brown cowboy hat were loaners from Tyler's closet.

"When in Montana…" he said.

Now that she was standing next to him, he could smell the sweet honeysuckle fragrance that he had come to associate with Josephine.

"You look uncomfortable." She laughed gently.

"I feel kind of uncomfortable," he admitted and tugged at the borrowed belt. "Maybe I should change."

"No. Don't change. You look good." She reached up and unbuttoned the top button of his shirt. "You just need to loosen up a little bit, that's all. You aren't on duty right now, so you don't have to have everything tucked in so tight."

Logan tugged at his shirt to loosen it per her instructions. He was used to having his shirts tucked to regulation uniform standards and it was hard for him to leave a button-down shirt loosely tucked. But if that was how

Josephine preferred it, he was willing to make the adjustment.

"How's that?"

"Good."

"Watch out for my girl, son." Hank had been watching them closely.

"And have a good time…" Barbara added.

They both said good-night to her parents before they met Jordan and Ian at the truck. Jordan got behind the wheel, Ian took shotgun, and Josephine climbed into the back of the cab with Logan.

Her sister put the key in the ignition. "Are you sure you don't want to drive, GQ?"

Josephine glanced over at Logan—he had noticed the unusual tension between Ian and Jordan, too.

"What's wrong?" Josephine asked her sister.

"Oh, nothing," Jordan said in a sarcastic, singsong tone. "Tyler thought it would be a good idea for Ian to drive the truck today when they were dropping hay for the cattle."

"Let it go." Ian used a low, stern tone with her sister that she had never heard before. It caught Josephine's attention—and like a child stuck in the middle of two parents, all she wanted to do was try to smooth things over between them.

"Come on, Jordy, don't spoil tonight over something petty."

"Petty?" Jordy retorted. "He *drove* the truck."

"He looks like he survived okay." Logan used his calm, even, de-escalation tone of voice.

"And Tyler wouldn't have done it if it wasn't safe," Josephine added on to what Logan had said.

Her sister's reflection in the rearview mirror was

stony. "Tyler thinks everything's a joke. I don't think this is funny."

"Hey…beautiful." Ian used a more conciliatory tone this time. "I'm okay. I wasn't in any danger. We were way out in the middle of nowhere—I couldn't've hit something if I tried. And you and I agreed…we *agreed*… that I needed to live my life. Take some risks. Not let my eyes hold me back…"

Josephine knew, and so did Logan and Ian, that behind her sister's anger was fear. She was afraid of Ian getting hurt. She was afraid of losing him, because she loved him so much.

"I've got to live, beautiful," Ian added gently. "You're the one who convinced me of that."

At the end of the long drive from the ranch house to the road, Jordan stopped the truck and looked over at her fiancé. "At least promise me you'll only drive in the fields."

"I swear on my honor as a Webelo." Ian leaned over to kiss her sister.

After they shared a kiss, Jordan explained, "Ian was a Boy Scout and he used that fact as a part of his strategy to woo me."

"You wanted me right from the start," Ian quipped.

"No. You wanted *me* right from the start, GQ. *I* thought you were a downtown wing nut."

That made Ian laugh, which completely broke the tension.

"You were there when they met, weren't you?" Josephine asked Logan.

"He was writing me a ticket!" her sister confirmed.

"Yeah…" Josephine gave Logan a wry look. "He does that a lot."

Josephine had never really enjoyed the trek from the ranch to Helena, not even when she was a little girl. Driving over hills and curves always made her feel carsick. But sitting in the backseat with Logan, who smelled so good and looked so handsome and seemed to like talking to her so much, she wasn't bothered by the trip this time. In fact, it seemed like the trip went by too quickly. She had been deep in the middle of a conversation with Logan about the skewed negative impact that the drug policy had on lower income and minority communities. The man was sharp, no doubt about it. And she had to admit that she had judged him harshly. She had always figured that he was a blue-collar guy who wouldn't be able to keep up with her or her friends in a conversation about political policy or law. She was seriously mistaken.

It had been a long time since she had line danced or had a beer. The idea of it was surprisingly appealing. Perhaps she had had one too many martinis.

It was the weekend, so the bar was crowded. They found an empty table near a small stage off the dance floor. Josephine wondered how Ian was handling the noise and the people—he didn't like crowds. But he was sitting close to Jordan with his hand on her leg, and he was smiling.

"I'm going to grab the drinks. What does everyone want?" Logan hadn't joined them at the table.

Josephine stood up. "I'll go with you."

They managed to squeeze into a tight space at the bar. The front of his body was touching the back of hers. From their harrowing experience in the cave, when he had rescued her and carried her to safety, she remembered how his body felt. At the time, she had been too frightened, and in too much pain, to appreciate the sheer maleness of the man. But later, when she was alone, and had time to reflect, she had spent quite a bit of time thinking about how strong he was, how feminine he made her feel when she was next to him.

They grabbed four beers and headed back to the table. Logan pulled her chair out for her before he took the chair next to hers. They tapped their four bottles together and toasted the wedding.

"How long has it been?" her sister asked her.

In unison, they said, "Prom."

She hadn't line danced since she was in high school, but when she saw the dancers all lined up, laughing while they moved through the repetitive steps, she wanted to join them.

"Do you mind?" Jordan asked Ian, who shook his head "no."

Her sister grabbed her hand and they went out onto the dance floor together. They danced for one song, and then had so much fun that they danced two more. Josephine was flushed and laughing when they returned to the table. She grabbed her beer off the table before she sat down. Two beers later, she was feeling warm all over, her lips were a little numb, and she was ready to get back out on the dance floor.

She held out her hand to Logan. "Are you coming, Lieutenant Wolf?"

Surprised by her question, Logan put his glass of water down.

"I owe you a dance, remember?" His hesitation made her regret the question. But when he stood up and took her hand into his, her regret was forgotten.

"I remember," Logan said.

It felt strange to hold his hand. It wasn't the hand she was used to. It was smaller, rougher, and stronger. And yet, it felt like a key slipping into a lock. A perfect fit. Perhaps even a perfect match.

They found a small area on the crowded dance floor where they wouldn't be in the way of the other couples. The music was blaring and Josephine had to nearly shout her words.

"Have you ever danced the Texas Two-Step?"

Logan leaned his head down. "No. I don't really dance all that much in public."

"Oh. Okay. Um…is it going to bother you if I have to take the lead position at first?"

"Bother me?"

"Well…embarrass you."

Logan smiled with just his lips, and gave a quick shake of his head. "No. Why?"

"Just checking."

Most of the guys she grew up with wouldn't let a woman take the lead position on the dance floor. Maybe in private, but not in public where their buddies could see them. It was a macho thing, she supposed. She wasn't all that surprised that Logan would let her take the lead—he was a masculine man, yes, but he didn't have a macho persona.

Josephine took the lead position, one hand in his, the other on his waist.

"Okay—let me think this out—when I step forward with my left, you step back with your left—no! Wait." She laughed. "I step forward with my *right* and you step backward with your left."

"Like this?" He asked.

"Yeah. And then it's step, step, feet together. Step, step, feet together. See how they're doing it?"

Logan watched the feet of the couples dancing around them. He had a feeling that he was about to make a total fool out of himself in front of Josephine, but he wasn't going to back out now. This was an opportunity to get close to her, to touch her, and be near her. If he looked like an idiot, so be it. He was just happy to have the excuse to have her in his arms.

"Ready?"

"Sure. Step, step…"

"Feet together," she said in unison with him.

He watched the couple that danced by and then said, "I think I've got it."

He didn't have it. He moved the wrong foot back and then when he moved the correct foot back, he forgot to put his feet together. While the other couples whirled by them, they had only covered a short distance in a choppy, uncoordinated way. When he managed to trip the both of them and they nearly landed in a heap in the middle of the dance floor, they both stopped because they were laughing too hard.

"This stupid dance is harder than it looks." Logan tilted his hat back a bit on his head.

"Why don't you try taking the lead this time?" she suggested. "Maybe that'll help."

"Do you really think anything will help me at this point?" he asked, smiling.

"Honestly? Probably not. But, a deal's a deal."

Logan laughed at her blunt assessment of his dancing ability. "Hey, if you're willing to stick it out with me, then I'm going to give it another try."

Logan took her back into his arms and took the lead.

In his head, he was thinking, *Step, step, feet together. Step, step, feet together.*

"Ow!"

"Oh, crap! I'm sorry, Jo!" Logan apologized when he stepped hard on her instep.

Josephine bent down and rubbed the top of her boot. It hurt. He had stepped down really hard on her foot, but instead of worrying about the pain, she was laughing. She had been laughing with Logan the entire time they had been on the dance floor. The man could not dance, but he was a lot of fun to be around.

"Are you okay?" he asked.

Still laughing, she nodded. "I'll be fine."

"I suck, don't I?" He was smiling now.

Josephine straightened upright, her foot still smarting a bit. "I'm sorry, but, yes, you really do..."

"Do you want to go back to the table?"

"Please."

He noticed that she was limping, just a little bit, when they walked back to the table.

"You're going to start thinking that I'm bad luck," he told her. "Every time I get near you, you end up getting hurt."

Josephine sat down. "Don't worry about it. I'll be fine."

"What happened out there?" Jordy asked them in good humor. "I told Ian that sometimes it's an advantage not to be able to see."

"Sucking that badly takes a lot out of you." Logan polished off the water left in his glass. "I thought I was going to have my John Travolta *Urban Cowboy* moment out there."

"From what Jordan told me, it was more like an urban train wreck out there," Ian said.

Josephine liked how easily Logan could laugh at himself. She had always appreciated that trait in other people, mostly because she didn't have that trait herself. She tended to be more self-conscious. She tended to be too much of a people-pleaser at times.

They had all discovered that Logan couldn't dance, but what he could do was sing. When the band took a break and the bar switched to karaoke, Logan put his name on the list. When he stepped onto the small stage, with his jeans and western-style shirt, and his charming smile, Josephine couldn't take her eyes off him. And she noticed she wasn't the only one. Like he was a country superstar, a small group of women gathered near the stage to hear him sing. Once the music started and he actually started to sing a popular country song, the crowd of women grew.

"Uh…*wow*!" Jordan swiveled her head around to look back at her. "Did you know that he could sing like that?"

Josephine didn't want to talk. She wanted to listen. She gave a quick nod of her head to her sister but kept her eyes on Logan.

"Did you know?" her sister asked Ian.

"Wolf was the lead singer for a band when we were in high school," Ian told them.

Logan's voice made chill-bumps pop up all over her body. His voice seemed to touch places *inside* of her body and made her feel the lyrics of the song as much as she heard them. Logan, with his stage presence, his looks, and his voice, could have been a professional singer. It made her curious about him. How had he ended up being a cop instead?

When he finished singing, everyone clapped. But the women near the stage clapped the loudest. One woman in particular, a pretty brunette wearing skin-tight jeans and tank top, approached Logan when he came off the stage. Josephine watched Logan bend down his head to talk to the petite woman. The uncomfortable, almost painful, sensation that shot through her body could only be described as good, old-fashioned jealousy.

Logan and the brunette actually looked good together as they walked together through the crowd toward the table. And she didn't like it. She didn't like how the woman reached out and touched Logan's arm now and again. She didn't like how overly friendly Logan was being.

"Everyone—this is Brandy. Brandy—everyone."

"Hi, y'all." Brandy gave a cute little wave. "Are you sure you don't want a shot? I'm buyin'."

"Thank you, Brandy. Maybe another time."

Maybe another time?

Logan should have given this Brandy chick the full-on boot.

"Okay, if you're sure." Brandy was staring up at Logan with open admiration. "I think you're an incredible singer. Are you coming back next weekend?"

"No," Josephine said this without thinking about it. "We're not."

Brandy looked at her as if she were noticing her for the first time. "Oh. Okay. Well…" Another cutesy wave. "See you around."

Logan said goodbye to his new fan and then moved his chair just a little closer to Josephine's chair before he sat down.

"Holy *crap*, Logan! You're frickin' amazing!" Jordy exclaimed.

"Thank you," he said humbly. "What did you think, Jo?"

When Josephine ran Brandy off, she gave him reason to hope. He had thought that this attraction was a one-sided affair. But now he was thinking that Josephine had started to think of him as more than just a friend.

"I think you're amazing," she told him. "I'd like to hear you sing again."

Logan signed up for another slot, but when his name was called a second time, Josephine heard her name called, too.

Logan stood up and held out his hand to her. "Come on, Jo. We're up."

"What?" Josephine asked, horrified. "No! I'm not going up there!"

Logan wouldn't take her "no" for an answer. He grabbed her hand, tugged her out of her seat, and led her up to the stage.

The lights hurt her eyes, but at least she couldn't see past the first row of women huddled near the front of the stage. Right before the music started, she tried to exit the stage, but Logan held on to her hand.

"I can't do this," she whispered harshly.

"Sure you can," he whispered back. "I picked our song."

In the next moment, Josephine heard the music for her favorite Judds song begin to play.

"Come on, Jo." Logan squeezed her fingers. "Sing a duet with me."

Josephine looked into Logan's rich, black eyes and what she saw in his eyes made her want to never look away. No man in her life had ever looked at her the way Logan was looking at her right now. And that was when she decided to stay on the stage with him.

"Okay…" she finally agreed. "But I'm Wynonna."

Chapter Eleven

It was a quiet trip back to the ranch. Josephine couldn't remember the last time she'd laughed so hard or had so much fun. The last several years of her life hadn't been about having fun. They'd been about getting her education and becoming the type of attorney who could make a difference in people's lives. She had literally let her hair down tonight. She'd put on her boots, drank more than a few beers, danced, and even sung karaoke with Logan three times. The first, Logan had basically pushed her onstage. The second and third time, she didn't need any pushing.

Josephine hugged her sister and her brother-in-law-to-be and then she was alone with Logan. It was after midnight and the ranch was asleep. For weeks, as her friendship deepened with Logan, she had always felt comfortable whenever she was with him. But standing with him now, she felt something shift inside of her body. Tonight, and truly for the first time, Logan seemed much more like a man who had captured a piece of her heart than a man who was only a friend.

Logan was grateful that Ian and Jordan had given him a chance to be alone with Josephine. Standing beside her, with the dark Montana mountains in the background, and bright yellow stars splashed across the blue-black sky, he wanted to kiss her. To his eyes, she was more beautiful tonight than any woman he'd ever seen. The gentle night air was blowing the loose, long strands of her hair around her face and shoulders. This woman was so pretty, so soft and sweet. He knew now that he wanted more from this woman than he had ever wanted from another woman.

"Well, good night." Josephine turned away from him, arms now crossed protectively in front of her body.

"I'll walk you back." Logan had almost built up the nerve to kiss her when she turned away from him.

Josephine started to walk quickly toward the porch. "You don't have to…"

"Yes, I do." He fell in beside her.

Josephine had been giving him green lights all night, but now, her body language was throwing up a giant stop sign. It wasn't the right time for a first kiss.

She flew up the stairs and it made him think that, like him, she had felt something change between them tonight. Up until tonight, Josephine had always treated him like a good friend. But when she chased Brandy away at the bar…that gave him hope—hope that a new spot had opened in her heart. A spot that he'd like to fill.

"Jo…"

At the top of the steps, Josephine stopped. The soft

moonlight made the long strands of her hair look like threads of gold blowing gently around her beautiful face. It was a face that he had grown to love.

"Look, I don't know where you are in your recovery, but do you want to go out on a date…with me?"

Josephine had felt in her gut that this question was coming. She had known, for a while, that Logan found her attractive—that he was interested—but until tonight, she had never encouraged him. She had always kept him a safe arm's length away. Her possessiveness at the bar, when she told Brandy to shove off, had surprised her. Yes, Logan was a nice-looking man. That was undeniable. But in most ways, he wasn't really her type. He was laid-back about life; he wasn't as driven to succeed in a career as she was. There were fundamental differences. Should she start something with a man that seemed destined to end? Or was a summer fling with a hot cop exactly what she needed?

"Okay." She agreed to the date. "When?"

"We're moving the chapel tomorrow, but I was planning on heading up to Flathead Lake for some snorkeling the day after next. Are you up for a little road trip?"

"Actually…" she said after a moment of hesitation, "I am up for it. Thank you."

"Then…it's a date?" Logan asked.

Standing on the porch stairs of her childhood home, with a full moon and the majestic mountains off in the distance, the romance of the moment didn't escape Josephine.

"Yes," she said quietly. "It is a date."

The day they moved the chapel down from the mountain was a crazy day at the ranch. Josephine's dress for the wedding, which should have arrived the week before, finally came. It seemed to be a day for arrivals, because her mom's horse, Rising Star, decided it was a good day to give birth to her foal. There was so much activity, with the extra men and equipment for the chapel move, and Josephine wanted to be out in the mix. Instead, she was inside of the house trying on the dress for the wedding. Normally, trying on a pretty dress would be a top priority, but today wasn't a normal day.

"It's too loose around the waist." Her mom clucked her tongue. "I told you that you looked like you were losing weight, Josephine. You're getting too thin."

"I'm not trying to lose weight." She spun around and looked at her reflection in the full-length mirror.

Her maid of honor dress was to-die-for. It was a floor-length gown with a straight silhouette and a completely sheer back. The fabric was dark purple, silk chiffon that made her look like she was floating when she walked.

"We're going to have to get it altered right away." Her mom pulled the fabric tighter around her waist to make it fit perfectly.

"What do you think, Jordy?" Josephine asked her sister.

"I think it's the perfect dress for you, Jo." Her twin nodded her approval. "You look like you just walked right off the catwalk."

Josephine twirled around in a small circle with a smile. She had intended to pass on this dress because it was so striking that she didn't want it to seem like she was trying to compete with the bride. But Jordan had insisted that this was the gown she would wear for the wedding.

"Why don't we plan on…" Her mom started to speak,

but a loud booming sound outside startled her and interrupted her sentence.

Barbara shook her head, her expression tense and irritated. "I am so *annoyed* with your father about this chapel business. That chapel has been sitting there for a hundred years, and this is the time to move it?"

"This is Dad's wedding present to me, Mom." Jordan looked up from her phone. "You should really give Dad a break."

"Jordan?" their mom asked. "Don't you have a painting to finish?"

"So, that's my cue to buzz off." Her twin laughed easily. "By the way, sis, I posted the pics from last night on Instagram."

Josephine shrugged her shoulders and made a face. "I've broken up with social media."

"Well, most people haven't, if you catch my drift. Chances are, the dingle-berry will see them."

"I doubt he'll care one way or the other," she said.

"Jordan, really," Barbara piped up. "Do you have to be so crass? You're about to become the wife of a very well-known man."

Jordan kissed her mom quickly on the cheek. "Trust me, Ian knows how I am and he loves me anyway."

"Go!" Barbara pointed to the door, half playful, half serious. "Paint!"

"Fine, I'm going. Ian and I are going up to check out how far along they are with the chapel."

After Jordy left, Josephine got out of the gown as quickly as she could. She agreed to eat a few more carbs before the wedding and her mom agreed to hold off on calling the seamstress. Once she was back in her boots and jeans, Josephine ran out the front door and walked quickly up the driveway. Her father had decided to relocate the chapel on top of a small hill that overlooked the farmhouse. Like a crown jewel, there would a bird's-eye view of Bent Tree Ranch from the chapel.

She could hear the voices of the men yelling back and forth, shouting instructions and words of caution as they moved the chapel up the hill to the new foundation. Josephine climbed up to the top of the hill and joined the crowd of people gathered there.

"Oh, my goodness…" She said to no one in particular. The sight of the chapel, now on the back of an enormous, specialized semitruck, was remarkable. She had thought it was an impossible task and would likely be the end of the chapel. But she was wrong. The truck with the intact chapel was creeping up the hill toward the spot where a foundation had been built.

"Pretty frickin' amazing, isn't it?" Jordan asked her.

"It's really something," she agreed.

Everyone was there. Tyler, Jordan, Ian, her dad. It didn't seem right that her mom wasn't here to witness this historic family event. But just as she was having that thought, her mom appeared from the other side of the hill. Josephine scanned all of the men who were working to find Logan. She didn't see him at first, but she heard his voice. When he appeared from the other side of the truck that was carrying the chapel, she smiled. That was her immediate, spontaneous reaction to seeing Logan again. A smile.

When Logan saw her, standing on the hill next to her parents, he smiled, broadly and freely. It was a brief, shared moment between them before he refocused his attention on the chapel. The move took all day, from sunup to sundown. And when the crew finally achieved its goal of relocating the chapel to its new foundation at the top of the rolling hill that overlooked the farmhouse and barns, everyone present felt like cheering. Once the chapel safely in place, Logan walked over to her father. The two men shook hands.

"That was an amazing thing to watch," Hank said to Logan. "I can't believe what you pulled off here, Logan. We couldn't have done this without you."

"It just took the right resources, sir," Logan said humbly.

"It was more than that," her father replied.

Her father admired Logan. He respected him. And it made her view Logan with a fresh perspective. She always dated tall. She was tall, her father was tall—everyone in her family was tall. So she gravitated toward tall men to date. She had always equated tall with masculinity and strength. But now, watching Logan with her father—even though he was shorter than Hank, he wasn't any less strong or masculine. Quite the opposite.

Her family had surrounded Logan like he was a rock star, thanking him and congratulating him. She hung back, feeling an unusual sense of shyness at the thought of coming face-to-face with him. And she knew that she hadn't felt this way for a man in a long, long time. She had only felt this way one time before in her life, and that was when she first met Brice.

And then he was in front of her, looking directly into her eyes. He was dirty and hot and his shirt was soaked with perspiration. And it didn't bother her.

"What do you think?" he asked her. He seemed to want her approval.

The truth was that she was close to tears—happy tears. In a sense, Logan had rescued the chapel. Without planning and without thinking, Josephine hugged him. And then she kissed him on the cheek.

"Thank you." She let go of him.

He stood there, silently staring at her, as if he had forgotten what he wanted to say. Finally, he asked, "Do you want to get a closer look at her?"

"Yes."

The whole family walked over to the chapel with them, and Logan explained what the next steps would be to make sure the structure was sound. Logan estimated that they would be able to begin remodeling the chapel within the next couple of days, and the exterior of the chapel, at least, would be ready for Jordan and Ian's pre-wedding session with the photographer. Slowly, after the initial excitement dissipated and evening chores called, the crowd of people dwindled. Josephine lingered. She wanted more time with the chapel. And she wanted more time with Logan.

She found a spot of ground and sat down. While she watched the hired crew gather their tools and load them onto their trucks, she pulled blades of grass free from the earth around her. When she found two rather long pieces of grass, she wrapped them around her finger and then started to tie them into a knot. Her eyes followed Logan as he went about his business. And, she noticed, when he was working, the man was *all* business. Much like the day she first met him, when he threw the book at her and gave her three tickets. Maybe he wasn't ambitious in the same way she was, but he was a hard worker. That was undeniable.

The last of the workers piled into their trucks and left. Logan walked over to where she was sitting and offered her his hand.

"Were you waiting for me?"

She nodded, wiped off the dirt and grass from the seat of her jeans.

"Thank you. You're a sweetheart."

It was dusk now and the full moon was rising over the mountain range in the distance. They were standing together, alone on the hilltop next to the chapel. And that was when she had an impulse. Perhaps it had been there for a while. Perhaps it was something entirely new. But one minute she was standing next to Logan, and then next minute she was in his arms, kissing him.

Logan had been up late the night before and up early in the morning. He was hot and hungry, covered in dirt and mud. He was exhausted. But when Josephine started to kiss him, all of that was forgotten. Her lips were soft, her skin was soft, and she felt so good in his arms. Their first kiss, a kiss he had been worrying about, was gentle and tentative and more meaningful than he had imagined. He held her face in his hands and kissed her lips lightly; she rested her hands lightly on his chest.

When the kiss ended, neither of them spoke. Neither of them moved. They stood facing each other, in the dusk, quiet with their own whirling, private thoughts.

She couldn't believe that she had done something so out of character as kissing Logan. But she had kissed him and she had liked it. It was exciting to kiss him. And it was exciting to have him kiss her back. His lips were strong, like the rest of him, but he was a surprisingly gentle kisser. And for the moment at least, she didn't regret stepping right over that friendship line. In fact, she was pretty certain that she intended to cross that line again.

Josephine heard the sound of the dinner bell and the silence between them, the spell, was broken.

"If we don't go down there, she'll just send up a posse to get us," she told him. "Are you hungry?"

"I'm pretty much always hungry."

As they started the trek down the hill together, Logan reached for her hand. His hand, so warm and strong and calloused, was starting to feel like a new normal. Holding Logan's hand was starting to feel like coming home.

"So…we're still on for tomorrow. Right? Snorkeling at Flathead Lake?"

"We're still on." Josephine didn't bother to hide her natural enthusiasm. She knew that she could be herself around Logan, without any pretense. "Actually, I can't wait."

Everyone in her family noticed that she was leaving for the day with Logan, but no one said a word against it. Perhaps they had all seen this coming, or perhaps they were just glad to see her with someone other than Brice. Either way, their quiet acceptance of the relationship, casual and fleeting as it would most likely be, was a relief. They took one of the ranch trucks and headed to the largest body of fresh water west of the Mississippi. Ever since Logan had seen a picture of Flathead Lake, which had gone viral, he had put it on his "must visit" list while he was in Montana.

They rolled the windows down, cranked up the tunes, and embarked on their first mini road trip together. The more she got to know Logan, the more relaxed she felt around him. He was a blast to be around. He wasn't uptight. He didn't have an agenda. He just wanted to have a good time and he wanted to get to know her better.

To have a hot guy, one that her family approved of, no less, interested in her, was a boost to her wounded ego. That was the truth. Why shouldn't she have a romantic summer? Why shouldn't she act on the attraction that Logan felt for her and she felt for him? She was no longer attached. She was free to date. She was free to kiss. She was free to make love…

Her cell phone rang. She pulled it out of the front pocket of her shorts and looked at the screen. She stared at the name, unbelieving.

Brice.

Logan glanced over at her. "Everything okay?"

She pushed the decline button and slipped the phone back into her pocket.

"Yeah," she said. "Everything is just fine."

When they arrived at the park, Logan found a parking spot and jumped out of the truck. Whenever he was getting ready to do something out-of-doors, whether it was hiking or going into the cave or snorkeling, Logan would act as excited as a little kid. He was animated and pumped up and ready to take everything in.

"Man, look at this place! I love it!" Logan immediately walked over to the rocky edge of the massive lake and looked around. "I've got to come back here and scuba dive. Do you ever scuba dive?"

"Uh-uh. No." She shuddered at the thought. "I have a really bad fear of drowning. I like to be near my air source at all times, thank you kindly."

Logan laughed. "But you will snorkel."

"Snorkeling's doable. Yes."

They grabbed their gear and staked out a spot on the man-made beach. Even in the summer, the temperature of the water was only seventy degrees at the surface.

They had brought wet suits so they could stay in the water for a longer period of time.

"I dare you to jump in." Josephine rubbed sunscreen on her face and neck.

"You're daring me?" Logan questioned her as if he had heard her wrong.

"That's right." She pulled her T-shirt over her head and exposed the top half of the Speedo she wore to swim laps. "I dare you."

Logan grinned at her, his eyes appreciative. "Child's play."

"We'll see," she egged him on.

Logan stripped off his top, and when he caught her openly staring at his beautifully developed torso, his smile widened.

"I like your tattoo," she said.

"I like you," he said easily. "Take off your shorts."

"Excuse me?"

"If I'm going in, so are you."

"So, wait a minute. Are you trying to dare me with my own dare?"

He nodded.

"Fine." Josephine took off her shorts, folded them neatly, and put them down on top of her folded T-shirt. "Montana woman." She pointed to herself and then pointed to him. "California boy. Who has the advantage?"

Logan looked down at her long, bare legs and his smile widened. She knew what he was thinking—he liked what he saw. "Well, I suppose we're about to figure that one out."

Without any warning, he scooped her up into his arms and carried her, legs flailing, mouth protesting, into the lake.

"Logan!" she commanded sternly. "Put me down!"

"In a minute." He kept on walking into the lake.

"*Not* in the water…on the *beach*!" she clarified her command.

"Sorry," he said easily. "No can do."

When he was waist-high in the water, Logan spun around and fell backward into the water, taking her with him. The minute they hit the water, he let her go. Her feet touched the lake bottom and she stood up. Being chest-deep in the frigid water felt like a thousand tiny needles were pricking her skin all over.

"Wooo!" Logan let out a loud whoop when he emerged from beneath the water and shook the water from his short black hair. "That's damn cold!"

"Ya think?" Josephine splashed water at him.

Logan only smiled in response, reached out and pulled her toward him. Before she could think to stop him, he kissed her. Right there, in Flathead Lake, he kissed her. The moment his warm mouth touched hers, she forgot all about being cold, she forgot about the small audience on the beach, and enjoyed the taste of the fresh lake water on Logan's lips.

Chapter Twelve

The trip to Flathead Lake marked a shift in Josephine's relationship with Logan. They left that morning as friends with potential for more. They returned to the ranch as two people who were more than "just friends." She never returned Brice's call. His message was vague, but she had a feeling that the only reason he had bothered to call was because he saw the pictures on Jordan's Instagram. That kind of attention she didn't need from him.

"Good afternoon, Lieutenant Wolf," Josephine greeted Logan when he walked into the barn.

"Hey."

Josephine latched the latch to the stall door. "Have you seen the new baby?"

"Not yet."

Logan stopped beside her, slipped his arm around her waist, pulled her to his side, and kissed her on the lips.

"How are you?" he asked.

"Good. Things are on track. No major issues or melt-downs in the wedding situation room." She liked how he would just grab her and kiss her. He was an affectionate man, more affectionate than she was used to. "I was just coming up to see you."

"I was looking for you," he said. "Were you heading up to the chapel?"

"Yes. Were you looking for cheap labor?"

"I was just hoping you'd improve the scenery," he said.

Logan admired the new colt for a moment before he turned around and leaned back against the stall. Over the weeks, he had started to look less like a San Diego police officer and more like a Montana cowboy. His hair had grown longer and curled out beneath his standard-issue cowboy hat. He had traded shorts and hiking gear for jeans and cowboy boots. He always had a pair of gloves tucked into his back pocket; his naturally golden skin had turned a dark brown around his neck and his forearms.

The more time she spent with this man, the more handsome he became. There was a kindness in his brown eyes and sincerity in his smile. He was a go-with-the-flow kind of guy; it was refreshing. For now, for a summer fling, he was perfect for her. And when he kissed her, like she could tell that he was about to do now, her body felt pleasure all the way from her lips to the tips of her fingers. Since their trip to the lake, there had been a whole lot of kissing. It was that sweet, often excruci-atingly slow, dance toward making love. Logan wasn't pushing her—if anything, she had been pushing him…a little bit further, a little bit further, every time they were able to steal away for a clandestine lovers' moment.

Logan was admiring her, as he always did, with his eyes. There was a small, intimate smile on his firm lips as he reached out to put his hands on either side of her slim hips. She took his hat off his head and put it onto hers.

"Can I have a minute of your time, cowboy?" she asked suggestively.

"You can have as many minutes as you want."

Josephine took his hand and led him over to a ladder that led up to the hayloft. She knew that he was staring at her derriere as she climbed up ahead of him. Enticing him, making him want her even more, was part of the plan. It was, she had recently discovered, part of the fun. She had been thinking about taking him up to the hayloft, something she had never done with a man, and today seemed like the perfect opportunity. They were the only ones in the barn—why not take advantage of the moment?

Logan knew what she wanted. He knew exactly what to do. When he joined her in the loft, he pulled a knife out of his front pocket, cut the twine off a fresh bale of green, sweet-smelling alfalfa hay, and spread the bale of hay over the old straw that was strewn across the wood floor of the loft.

Together, they lay down on top of the hay, facing each other. His eyes were smiling at her when he tucked a loose strand of hair behind her ear. He brushed his thumb over her lips, and then kissed her. Slow and gentle, that was how he always kissed her. She knew there was more behind those kisses, more to be discovered, but he held that part back. He was teasing her, in his way, building her anticipation, and driving her to come back to him for more. And it was working. She did want more. Her body wanted more.

Logan rolled her onto her back and then, for the first time, his body was on top of hers. His welcome weight pressed her down into the hay while his welcome lips left a trail of feathery kisses over her face and down her neck.

She couldn't help herself. She couldn't stop herself as she dug her fingertips into the muscles of his back, entwined her legs with his legs, and made a sound, a sound she had never made before. It was the sound of need. The sound of frustration. She knew her mind wasn't ready for them to make love, but her body was ready.

Logan lifted his head, put his hands on either side of her face, and dropped his hips down to hers so she could feel him. So she could feel the need she had created in him.

"Josephine…" The way he said her name, with so much reverence and care, let her know that she meant more to him than just a moment of a physical gratification.

Their eyes met and Logan shook his head as a private thought passed through his mind. "My God… Josephine…" He said gruffly. "Do you have any idea how beautiful you are to me?"

They kissed again, more deeply and longer than they had ever kissed before. She took his tongue into her mouth, just as she knew that she would soon take his body into hers. Logan broke the kiss, buried his face into her neck, and ground his hips into hers.

Josephine closed her eyes and enjoyed the feel of him. She loved the feel of his muscular arms and his muscular chest. From the very core of her body, a wonderful tingling spread. In her mind, she started to think—

Could I have an orgasm like this? Could I have an orgasm like this?

Usually, everything had to be *just right* for her to experience an orgasm. The lighting had to be right, the position had to be just right...

Yet there was a demanding ache between her thighs now, and she knew, unbelievably, that she was about to climax with Logan.

"Don't hold it back," he whispered in her ear.

She was too far gone in the moment to feel embarrassed that he *knew*. Logan's hands lifted her into his body and he took her higher and higher and higher until her head dropped back into the hay and she could sense an orgasmic moan rising from the back of her throat. She was so close...so close...

And then she heard her brother's voice.

Josephine's mouth clamped shut, her eyes popped open, and she stopped moving. She tightened her arms around Logan so he would stay still, too. They looked at each other, shocked that they were no longer the only ones in the barn. Once she knew that Logan was going to be quiet, she pushed on his shoulder to get him to move off her. Logan rolled carefully to the side. Josephine rolled onto her side and then got onto her hands and knees. She peeked through a gape in the floor and spotted her brother kissing London the intern.

Josephine scrunched up her face, sorry that she had witnessed a private moment between Tyler and London, while she lowered herself down onto her haunches. She shook her head at Logan and put her finger to her lips.

Logan, she noticed, looked like he needed to sneeze.

He was pinching his nose in an attempt to stifle it. She shook her head at him again and mouthed the word "no." The last thing she wanted was for Tyler to catch her in the hayloft with Logan. She'd never live that one down with her brother.

While Logan made a valiant attempt to stifle his sneeze, she listened carefully for voices. Finally, she heard her brother say something to London, and she was glad that she couldn't make out the words. It was bad enough she had seen the kiss! From her vantage point in the loft, she saw Tyler leave. And then she heard the sound of the office door at the other end of the barn shut. London had gone into the office, which gave them a window of opportunity to make their escape.

Josephine grabbed the discarded hat and quickly stood up. "Time to get out of Dodge."

Right after Logan stood up, the sneeze he had been holding back came out.

"Bless you," she whispered.

"Thank you." He got the two words out and then sneezed again.

"Bless you," she repeated.

Once he started sneezing, he didn't stop. He sneezed again, and again, and then again. He sneezed so many times that she stopped saying "bless you," just so he wouldn't have to try to say "thank you."

She wanted to tell him to walk and sneeze at the same time so they could make a clean getaway, but she didn't have the heart to do it. His eyes were red and swollen and his nose was clogged. He looked miserable.

"I think…" he said between sneezes, "that I'm allergic to the hay."

She nodded. The romantic scene had taken a rather

comical turn, and it hit them both at the same time. They started to laugh. And the more Logan sneezed, the more they laughed.

"Come on…" Josephine said to him. "Let's get you out of here."

Down the loft ladder, and out of the barn, they managed to leave undetected. Logan was still sneezing. He'd stop for a minute and it seemed like he was done, and then he'd sneeze again.

"Quit it." Logan ordered his sneezing to stop, but his body didn't listen. He kept right on sneezing for another couple of minutes.

"Holy mackerel," he said when the sneezing finally stopped. "I think next time we need to stay away from the hay."

"Agreed." She laughed.

Logan looked her over. "You have hay in your hair. And on your pretty little backside."

Josephine pulled her ponytail over her shoulder and picked the hay out of it. Then, she brushed off the seat of her jeans. She twirled around.

"Evidence gone?" she asked.

"You're good," he said. "How 'bout me?"

"I think we need to find you a Benadryl ASAP." She started to smile again.

He was smiling, too. He looked around to make certain that no one else would hear him. "I did enjoy the roll in the hay…"

His voice sounded different because his nose was completely clogged.

"Me, too," she agreed. "Until my brother interrupted us and all of the soft tissue in your noggin swelled."

"That wasn't sexy," he conceded with a self-effacing smile.

"Let's go ask Mom if she has an antihistamine, okay?"

Her mom did have the antihistamine. Josephine got the pills, poured a glass of water, and then handed them both to Logan.

"Thank you," he said after he took the pills and gulped down the water.

After she doctored him, Logan told her that he needed to go back to the chapel. Josephine wanted to stay behind and get some reading done, so she walked out to the front porch with him to say goodbye.

Logan paused on the top step. "Listen…I'm planning a trip up to the Continental Divide. I'm thinking that I'll be up there camping for about a week. If you think your mom and Jordan can spare you, I'd like you to come with me."

And there it was…the opportunity that they both knew they had been thinking about, the opportunity to be alone, the opportunity to make love.

Was she really ready for that? Were her mind and heart healed enough to take that permanent step away from Brice and into Logan's arms?

"What do you think?" he asked.

"I think…" she said thoughtfully, "that if my mom and Jordan can spare me, I'm going with you up to the Continental Divide."

Later that day, after she had spent several hours reading, Josephine strolled up the hill to the chapel. Logan was on the roof of the chapel, stripped down to a ribbed, white tank undershirt, his tanned skin soaking in the late afternoon sun. He wasn't tall, which still bothered her, but what he lacked in height, he made up in pure strength. She had never seen such an incredibly built male physique up close. This was the kind of body that men had in the movies or magazines. They rarely existed in real life.

Logan spotted her coming up the hill. He waved and climbed off the roof.

"Hey..." He met her halfway. "I was hoping you'd come to check out the progress."

Josephine couldn't believe the change in the chapel. Logan had dedicated most of his free time to refurbishing the old family landmark. Yes, he had help from various hands on the ranch, and everyone in the family had pitched in, but Logan was the driving force behind the project. She didn't understand why he had put most of his vacation plans on hold to rehab the chapel, but she was grateful.

"It's incredible, Logan. Better than I ever imagined."

"I wanted to make sure that at least the outside is done by the wedding."

"Jordy was hoping that the inside would be done, too..."

"I know...but that's not going to happen. Honestly, I'm pretty surprised that we've almost got the outside squared away."

"What you've managed to do is a miracle. I never imagined—I don't know that any of us ever really imagined—that the chapel would get a new life. I think we had all kind of given up on it."

"No..." Logan's eyes were on the chapel. "You should never give up on something that you love."

He continued to look at the chapel, his eyes seeming to take inventory of all the details that still needed to be tackled. She looked at him. The profile of his face was strong and handsome, but there were deep lines around his eyes from smiling and squinting, and the nose had a bump on the bridge that made him look like a prize fighter who had taken one too many hits to the nose.

"How are you with a brush?" He turned toward her and caught her staring at him.

"Not bad," she said. "I can hold my own."

Logan handed her a brush and put her to work. He cranked up the CD player because he knew that she liked the Temptations. While he painted, he sang to her. Every once in a while, she joined in, singing with him—with Logan, she felt like singing again. And he encouraged it; he enjoyed the sound of her voice.

When the song "My Girl" began, Logan laid down his brush, took the brush from her hand, led her to a grassy spot nearby and took her into his arms. On the hilltop, with the chapel as their backdrop, he held her in his arms and sang to her.

She loved it. She did. But it also made her feel embarrassed and shy. He was so open about his feelings. He liked her, he wanted to sing to her, and so he did.

"What are you doing?" she asked, looking around for someone who might see them.

"Dancing with my girl…" He sang the words "my girl."

"I thought you couldn't dance…" Was she his girl? She wasn't sure about that.

"I can't," he admitted. "But I can sway back and forth like this. And I can dip you…" He surprised her by dipping her over his arm and then swinging her back up.

"Come on, Jo…" Logan said, still holding her in his arms. "It's okay to have a good time, you know. No one's going to see you. It's just you and me up here."

He was right. And so she danced with him. On the hill, in front of the chapel, with Logan singing the Temptations to her…she danced.

At the end of the song, Logan dipped her one last time and when he brought her up, he ended their dance with a quick kiss. Once the dance was done, they went back to their painting. Josephine still couldn't quite figure Logan out—and she told him as much.

"You were so…serious that first day that I met you."

"You mean the day that I pulled you over and wrote you several tickets?"

"And probably jacked up my insurance premium…" she added.

"I was on duty," he explained. "I have to be different when I'm in uniform."

"Do you want to climb up the ranks? Be a police chief?"

"Why do I sometimes feel like I'm on a job interview with you that's not going so well?" he asked. "To answer your question, I don't want to climb up the ranks. I'm happy with what I'm doing. And I want to retire when I'm young enough so I can do what I really love to do."

"Which is?"

"Working with kids…troubled youth. That's their label, but I know there's a lot more to them than that label."

"I think that's admirable."

"I got involved with the Big Brothers program a couple years after I joined the force."

"You're a Big Brother?"

"Yeah, I love it." Logan put his paintbrush down so he could pull his wallet out of his back pocket. He flipped the wallet open and showed her one of the pictures inside.

"Javier's school picture," he told her. "He's a big boy for eight, isn't he?"

She nodded, then pointed to another picture. "Who's that?"

"That's Mom."

"Red hair."

"Yeah. My dad, my biological dad—not my stepfather, whom I call 'Dad'—was a full-blooded Choctaw Indian. Got my coloring from him. Didn't get much else."

Josephine stared at Logan curiously. There was so much about this man that she didn't know, yet she had nearly lost control of her reason and made love to him in the barn loft earlier that day. If Tyler hadn't interrupted them, could she really say that she wouldn't have gone there with Logan?

No.

"You're a Big Brother, and you're fifty percent Native American. I didn't know any of that about you."

Logan read between the lines of her statement.

"And that bothers you...that you don't know everything about me."

It was a statement, not a question.

"Yes. I suppose it does. In a way, we've crossed a few boundaries lately."

Logan stopped painting and put down his brush. His arms were crossed in front of his body, which was a protective stance that she wasn't used to seeing from him.

"Let me ask you this...and you don't have to answer me. Just be honest with yourself about it. Did you really know everything there was to know about that guy Brice?"

Chapter Thirteen

The morning that they were set to leave on their camping trip, Josephine headed to the barn to meet Logan. Jordan and her mom assured her that everything for the wedding was under control, so she decided to go on an adventure. When she arrived at the barn, she wasn't surprised that London already had two horses saddled for them and Easy Does It the mule was packed with supplies.

"Really?" Josephine asked when she saw her nemesis in mule form. "This was our best option?"

London patted the mule on the neck. "I had a talk with him and he assured me that he's up for the task."

Logan turned the corner carrying his rucksack. "Morning."

"We have to rethink this whole scenario," Josephine told him.

"What's the problem?" Logan packed his bag on the back of the mule.

Josephine pointed silently to Easy.

"She's holding a grudge against Easy," London, who was mucking out a nearby stall, said to him.

"Heck, yeah, I'm holding a grudge! He left me stranded...*twice*! I am not going all the way up to the divide only to have him take off with our coffee."

"Coffee?" Logan laughed. "Is that all you're worried about?"

"I have to have coffee first thing in the morning. It's non-negotiable."

"We need a strong, sure-footed pack mule and he's the best one we've got. We need him. Haven't you ever heard the phrase 'the third time's the charm'?"

In the end, Josephine conceded that they needed the mule for the trip, but she was holding Logan directly responsible for him. After they ran through their extensive checklist for the trip one last time, they set off on their journey. Logan had the trip planned out to the smallest detail. Planning for a camping trip to a high altitude location like the Continental Divide was something that Logan took very seriously. In this, he was not easygoing or go-with-the-flow. He knew it could be dangerous, so he tried to anticipate all of their needs. She had just basically needed to show up with her clothing and toiletries and get on her horse.

They stopped at the first camping sight, a spot on the ranch that her family had used over the years, in the early afternoon. Logan's plan called for them to take two slow travel days up to the peak, an overnight at the peak, and then two days for the return leg of the journey. She liked the slow pace that Logan had set for them. It forced her to relax and enjoy the moment. It forced her to get out of her own head, something that was very difficult for her to do.

"Do you know how to pitch a tent?" Logan asked her after he had unpacked the mule.

"Do I know how to pitch a tent? Does a duck like water?"

She had grown up on this land, surrounded by ranch hands, brothers, and a sister who was a tomboy. The only truly feminine influence on the ranch had been her cosmopolitan mother. She knew how to shoot a gun, fish, pitch a tent—she could even castrate a bull if she needed to get it done. It had been a long time since she had tapped into her inner woods-woman, but she was there.

Logan watched Josephine grab her tent and haul it over to a spot nearby. She had basically told him to mind his own business when he had offered to help her pitch her tent. When he had first met her, she was dressed like a fashionable, professional woman, with a designer dress and high heels. Now, she was in slim-fit jeans, boots, a button-up shirt with long sleeves rolled up to the elbow. Her long hair, hair that he loved to touch, was braided tightly into a thick braid down her back. Surprising to him, she now wore a large buck knife on her belt. He liked her in her business attire, but he really liked this side of her, too. He tried not to be too obvious about it, but it was hard for him not to stare at her long legs and shapely derriere in those jeans. He felt so attracted to this woman that it made him nervous. There had been no promises between them, no talk of continuing their relationship once they returned to California. Yet he had already, unintentionally, lost his heart to her. The question remained, was that a mistake?

Once she got started, her dormant camping skills

came right up to the surface and she pitched her tent more quickly than Logan pitched his. She stood proudly next to her tent.

"Do you need some help over there?" she teased him.

"No, I got it," Logan said. "Thank you."

Josephine smiled at the rare display of Logan's fragile male ego. While he finished pitching his tent, Josephine went on the hunt for some kindling to start a fire. Logan was finished with his tent when she returned with a pile of dried sticks in her arms.

"Coffee?" she asked.

"Absolutely," Logan said. He had already started to assemble his fishing rod. They had agreed that they both preferred to eat freshly caught fish for dinner while they were on the trip.

"I'm going to head down to the stream. You good?"

"There'll be coffee when you get back. Catch something good. I'm starved."

When he returned to the campsite, he had caught something good.

"Look at the size of this guy!" Logan showed her his catch—a massive trout.

"I'd forgotten how big they could get up here," she said, impressed. "I hope you're hungry too, so this doesn't go to waste."

Without hesitation, she took the fish, put it on a makeshift cutting board and started to clean it. Logan, who usually dated women who liked the outdoors, had never been with a woman who would clean a fish just as soon as she would get a French gel manicure. It caught him off guard so much that he simply stood there and watched her.

Josephine used a sharp filleting knife to cut open the

fish and in one easy, practiced motion, she gutted the fish. When she looked up from her task, bloody knife in one hand, fish head and spine in the other, Logan was staring at her with an odd expression on his face.

"Are you horrified?" she asked.

"No. Impressed."

"Oh…well, I know my way around a campsite."

"I'm picking that up," he said.

She put the head of the fish down and put the edible portion into a cast-iron skillet.

"Do you want to do the honors, or should I?" she asked.

He took the heavy skillet in one hand. "I'll cook it. You already did the dirty work."

That night, they sat by the fire, stuffed from the freshly caught and cooked fish dinner and several cups of strong, black campfire-brewed coffee. Perhaps it was the caffeine in the coffee, or perhaps it was the feeling of privacy and seclusion that being in the mountains created, but once Josephine started talking, she didn't stop. Not for a long time. She never used to talk very much with Brice. She had always thought that he was brilliant and what he had to say somehow mattered more than voicing her own thoughts. But with Logan—she liked to tell him what she was thinking. How she was feeling.

The moon overhead, nearly a full moon, was glowing large and bright in the expansive indigo sky. Josephine leaned her head back so she could stare up at that magical moon.

"I've always loved the moon," she told him. "My mom always stands under a full moon to get a moon kiss."

Logan liked to hear Josephine's thoughts. He liked to listen to the sound of her voice, to watch her facial expressions and the way her lips moved when she talked. No matter what time of day it was, he thought she was beautiful. To him, she was beauty personified. The firelight, and the light from the moon, only enhanced her natural beauty.

Silently, he stood up and extended his hand to her. She took it and he helped her stand up. Without pretense, he kissed her. He encircled her body with his arms, pulled her in, and gave her a sweet, gentle kiss. When he felt her arms tighten around his waist, when he felt her body sway into his, he deepened the kiss. His tongue danced with hers, one hand on her lower back, the other hand cradling her head.

Josephine loved Logan's kisses. She waited for them, looked forward to them. But even though he never hid his desire from her, he always held back. He had never tried to fondle her breasts or slip his hands between her thighs. There was a line he refused to cross. Even when she crossed that line, cupping the hard-on that was pressing against the material of his pants, he always kept his hands in "safe zones." His kisses, perhaps deliberately on his part, always left her wanting. Always left her needing more. Tonight was no exception.

Logan wasn't playing a game. He wanted her to come to him. He refused to push her into a sexual relationship with him. When it happened, it would be because *she* was ready. And it was not like she hadn't thought about it. She had. The idea of making love with Logan was very appealing. She knew the feel of his hard shaft through his clothes, but she had imagined what it would feel like, skin on skin, to hold him in her hands, to take him into her mouth—to have him inside of her body. She wanted that. And she had come close that day in the barn when she had almost let her libido take over. But perhaps that moment scared her, because they hadn't been that close since.

Just outside of her tent, Logan stopped to give her an enticing good-night kiss. Did she wish, in a way, that he would have at least *tried* to talk her into his sleeping bag? Yes. But that wasn't Logan's style. When it came to sex, she was the one who was in control. And even though it was an unspoken desire between them to make love on this trip, she still wasn't certain that she would.

"Good night, Jo." Logan's lips lingered on hers on last time, his fingertips touching her face.

"Good night." She unzipped the flap of her tent. "5:30?"

"5:30," he said. He waited for her to duck inside of her tent and zip it shut, and then she heard his tent flap zip shut.

Josephine climbed into her sleeping bag, but didn't fall asleep right away. She tossed and turned and kicked at her sleeping bag and pushed on her pillow. She couldn't get comfortable, but not because she was sleeping on the ground. She couldn't get comfortable because she was sexually frustrated and conflicted. She was having a silent debate, in her tent, in the dark. Should she get up and go to Logan's tent? She knew he would unzip his sleeping bag and welcome her without question. And, after much debate, she actually kicked her legs out of her sleeping bag, unzipped her tent and took a step toward Logan's tent. But then she heard the soft sound of his deep breathing, signally that he was already asleep. Obviously, he wasn't as bothered by his frustration as she was, and that made her doubt getting out of her sleeping bag in the first place. Quietly, she turned around, went back to her tent and crawled back into her sleeping bag. It wasn't the right time; it wasn't the right night. Perhaps it never would be.

The next morning they broke camp early and headed to their second camp location farther up the mountain. They both liked to ride in silence, enjoying the sounds of nature surrounding them that could only truly be appreciated if talking was kept to a minimum. They stopped for lunch, and to water the horses and the mule, and then they were back on the trail. Very quickly, they established a system for their trip, one that worked for them both. As with the first day of the trip, they made camp in the late afternoon so they could prepare the campfire for dinner, make a fresh catch, and make the sure the horses and Easy Does It were well rested for the toughest part of the climb to the peak.

As with the night before, Logan caught the fish, she cleaned it, and he cooked it. They had piping hot coffee after dinner and toasted marshmallows, toasted on a stick Logan carved for her. It was, in her memory, one of the best nights she had ever had. There was an easiness to their relationship, with the way they moved around the camp, that made her feel like she was part of a couple that had been married for years. It was the kind of easiness she saw with her parents, as if they could read the other's thoughts and anticipate the needs of the other without words. How had she managed to achieve this with Logan, a virtual stranger, when she hadn't managed to achieve it with a man she had been with for over five years? If she had been able to carry out her plan to marry Brice, would she have *ever* achieved that with him? Why had she been so willing to settle for less than the relationship she had always wanted just because she had put so much time into the relationship and Brice fit the criteria she had created in her mind about what "husband material" should look like? It scared her, and shook her confidence, to think how close she had come to possibly making a major life mistake. She went to sleep that night, with the very real awareness that marrying Brice would have been exactly that—a major life mistake.

After they broke camp the morning they were going to make the trek up to the Continental Divide, Logan checked the girth on her saddle and lifted the stirrup length on both of her stirrups before he tended to his own horse. This morning, more so than any other morning, Logan was focused and had few words to say. She knew why—this leg of the journey could be treacherous. They had to be prepared. They had to respect the climb they were about to ask their horses to make. The ascent to the divide would take them up another eight thousand feet. The air was thinner, which would make it harder to breath, and the temperature would drop thirty degrees. Cell phone service for emergencies would be limited to none.

Josephine had a jacket and a long-sleeved thermal shirt rolled up behind her saddle. By noon, even with the sun heating up the day, she would need to start adding layers as they made the climb. She mounted her horse and waited for Logan to swing into his saddle. He was a skilled horseman, and she could appreciate how he handled his horse and sat the saddle. She had confidence in him and his ability to safely lead them up the steep incline to their next campsite.

"Are you ready?" Logan used the reins to turn his horse to the left so he could look at her.

"Ready."

She wasn't a nervous rider, but she had been raised to respect the steep, tricky footing of the trail as they climbed closer and closer to the peak of the divide. At the halfway point, they stopped to take a break from the saddle and used the water from their canteens to water the horses and the pack mule. She was relieved that Easy Does It had willingly carried their equipment up the mountain without any protest. She had to give the little mule credit—he was getting the job done and he was doing it well.

Josephine pulled on her thermal shirt and the jacket because the temperature had already dropped nearly twenty degrees, according to the thermometer she had hanging off her saddle. After she zipped her jacket, she yawned loudly. She wasn't tired, so the need to yawn was a direct result of the air being thinner. When she breathed in the cooler air, she started to cough.

"Are you okay?" Logan was also slipping on a jacket.

"It's the asthma. I have my inhaler."

"Best use it now," he said.

Josephine took a couple of quick puffs from her rescue inhaler and then they were back in the saddle. They both were anxious to get to the next campsite. Even though the scenery was majestic, from spotting wildlife along the way to the unusual foliage, they both respected the dangers of the journey. They climbed higher and higher, and it grew colder and colder, until they reached an altitude that was as high as the clouds.

She had last made this climb with her brother Daniel when she was in middle school, and she was relieved when they finally reached the peak of the mountain they were scaling and found flatter terrain. The air was very thin now, and it was very cold, and Josephine started to realize that the mild case of asthma she had developed in her early adult years was making it difficult to breathe now that they were at the peak.

"Do you think we're close?" she called to Logan, who was a little bit ahead of her.

Logan stopped his horse and Easy Does It, and waited for her to catch up with him.

"I think the spot I picked out is just up ahead. What's wrong?"

"It's a little tough for me…to breathe."

"Can you make it, or do you need a break?"

"I think I can make it. If it's just around the corner like you said." The idea of a break didn't appeal to her. She wanted to get to camp, get the fire going, and get some hot coffee into her body.

"It's close," he assured her. "What do you want to do?"

By her choice, they kept moving. And Logan had been right—they were close. When they reached their destination, Logan grabbed a blanket from one of the saddlebags and wrapped it around her shoulders. He insisted that she sit down and conserve her breath while he made the fire. Once the fire was made, he settled her near it to keep her warm and put on the coffee. While she stayed warm by the fire, Logan quickly unloaded the horses and the mule and started the task of pitching the tents.

"We only need one," she told him. Her voice was weaker than normal, and he didn't hear her. She cleared her throat and said the words again, louder this time.

"Logan, we only need one tent tonight."

Logan straightened upright, her tent in his hands, and looked at her.

"Are you sure?"

She nodded her head in response.

Logan's eyes narrowed slightly as he contemplated her for a couple of seconds. Then he nodded one quick nod, put her tent down, and turned his attention to pitching his tent. *Their* tent. After he set up camp, he joined her near the fire. He poured them both a cup of hot coffee and joined her beneath the blanket. They sat together, quietly, at what seemed to be the top of the world.

"You can read about this. You can look at pictures." Logan looked off into the distance at the massive peaks that surrounded them for as far as the eye could see. "But actually being here...that's something else entirely."

Unexpectedly, without warning, tears began well up behind her eyes. Thoughts of her brother Daniel were so strong up here. Thoughts of the relationship—a friendship, really—that she had lost with Brice seemed more acute. Two men, two losses. She had no idea why it was hitting her so strongly right then, at that moment...but she was grateful that Logan was by her side and she was glad that he was so focused on the magnificent views that he hadn't noticed that she was fighting to hold back tears.

The weather, which had been in their favor for the first half of the trip, took a turn for the worse and forced them to go inside of the tent much earlier in the evening than they would have wanted. Logan had unzipped both of the sleeping bags completely and then laid them out like a makeshift mattress. They took off their jackets but left the rest of the clothing on. They lay down face-to-face and covered themselves with one of the sleeping bags and the blanket. Once they got situated, they looked at each other and started to laugh.

"It's damn cold up here." Logan reached out to pull her closer to him.

"The rain is making it colder…"

"How are you feeling? Better?"

Josephine nodded with a small smile. "I think I just needed a minute to adjust to the altitude."

"It's thin up here, that's for sure. It's tough for me, too."

"Logan?"

"Yes?"

"How do you feel about spooning?" she asked.

"Are you still cold?"

"Freezing."

"Then, come here, baby…I'll warm you up." He scooted backward as far as he could so she could turn into his arms. He wrapped her up tightly in his warm arms and she immediately felt better.

"How's that?" he asked. "Better?"

She nodded again, but had another question. "Logan?"

"Yes, sweetheart?"

"Why haven't you tried to make love to me?"

Logan's body grew still; she could feel his strong heart beating against her back. "I was giving you space."

Josephine spun around again, snuggled into his body and hooked her calf around his lower legs.

She looked directly into his eyes and asked, "What if I don't want the space anymore, Logan? What then?"

Chapter Fourteen

Her words were the green light Logan had been waiting for. He got rid of his clothes while she disrobed beside him. He was already aroused, and had been since they first lay down together. Now he just needed her body. But he knew that he wanted more than just her body— that was why he had waited for her. And the fact that there was a persistent voice in the back of his mind that was wondering if *she* wanted more from him than only a summer fling.

He rolled her gently onto her back and leaned on his arm to look down into her pretty, oval face. He didn't see doubt or hesitation in her light blue eyes—he saw desire. Pure desire, for him. He kept them both covered, he wanted to continue to keep her warm, but he needed to touch her. He had wanted to touch her for so long. He started at her lips, running his finger lightly over them, before he let his fingertips trail down the side of her face, to her soft neck, and down to her small, round breasts. He covered one breast with his hand, massaging it, teasing the hardened, sensitive nipple. Josephine closed her eyes, and Logan heard her sigh at the touch of his hand on her flesh. She was ready for the next step. She was ready for him.

Logan wanted to take his time exploring her body with his hands and she let him do it. Her skin was so silky and smooth, her legs and body so slim and finely muscled. He ran his hand along the side of her hip, down her leg, and then moved it back up. Without him having to say a word, Josephine opened her thighs, just a little, just enough, for him to slip his hand between them. She was wet, so wet, that he had to close his eyes, drop his head, and stop his own need to drive him to rush them to a quick release. He had waited too long for this to end quickly. He lowered himself down beside her, kissed the side of her neck, as he slowly slipped his fingers inside of her.

"Oh..." Josephine's head tilted back when he pushed his fingers deep inside of her. She reached down between them, encircled his thick shaft with her cool fingers.

He kept his fingers deep inside of her tight, wet center and worried her swollen clit with his thumb. She started to writhe against his hand, and bore down on his fingers, tighter and tighter, until she gasped loudly and her orgasm rained down on his fingers. His body wanted the same release he had just given her. But he made himself wait. There was only going to be one first time with his beloved Josephine and he had to make it count. He had to be the best she had ever had. He wanted her to believe, because it was true, that he was the best she ever *would* have.

Logan moved on top of her, but instead of entering her, as she might have anticipated, he moved downward, positioning his shoulders between her thighs with his hands beneath her tight rear end. Again, she didn't resist him. She welcomed him, relaxing her thighs and lifting her body upward to meet his mouth. Josephine dragged her fingers through his hair and it pleased him to hear how loudly she gasped when his tongue slipped inside of her. When he tasted the sweet aftermath of her orgasm, Logan growled low in his throat and lost himself in the feast. When Josephine's thighs tightened against his shoulders, her fingers pressed the back of his head into her core, and her fresh cries of release filled the small tent, Logan couldn't wait any longer. He quickly rolled on a condom and repositioned himself between her thighs.

Josephine looked up at him, a mixture of surprise and such uncertainty, that he almost stopped. But then she raised her hips upward, seeking, wanting, and that was the only encouragement he needed. With his hands positioned on either side of her shoulders, Logan locked his eyes with hers as he connected their bodies together.

Logan seated himself completely within her slick center. He closed his eyes so he could focus on the incredibly feeling of being joined with Josephine. She was a perfect fit for him. She was tight, and hot, but deep enough to take all of him inside of her. He pulled out of her slowly, torturing himself, then sank back into her again and again and again. Josephine's hands were on his chest, and the faster his rhythm became, the more she dug her fingernails into his skin. God help him, he felt her tighten around him and it drove him wild. His pace was frantic, crazy, driving into her harder and faster until she screamed his name. The sound of his name on her lips—that was the trigger that made him explode. One last hard thrust, he climaxed and, as if wrenched from his heart, he shouted her name.

"Josephine!"

After they made love, they had fallen asleep in each other's arms. It was cold inside of the tent, but beneath the sleeping bag and thick blanket, and with Logan's body generating heat, she awakened hot and sweaty. Still naked, Josephine carefully slipped out from underneath Logan's heavy arm and stood up. Bent over, she tiptoed in the dark, trying not to step on Logan's legs, and unzipped the tent flap. She stepped outside into the frigid air. Barefoot and without clothing, Josephine walked a few steps away from the tent. Tonight was the full moon. The ground felt hard and crunchy and stabbed at the tender skin of her feet, but it didn't stop her from walking toward the bright moon in front of her that seemed so close to the mountaintop that she could reach out and touch it with her hand. She found a soft, grassy spot. She stopped, lifted up her arms as if she were flying, and spun around in the moonlight.

Logan awakened and it registered, immediately, that Josephine was gone. He riffled in the dark until he found the lamp and switched it on. He yanked on his shirt, his pants, and stuffed his feet into his boots without socks. The tent was unzipped, and he noticed that her jeans were still folded neatly by the open flap. He stepped out of the tent; his breath curled out of his mouth like he had just exhaled smoke from a cigarette. He almost turned around to grab his coat from inside of the tent, but then he saw Josephine, naked, twirling in the moonlight, and he temporarily lost his ability to move. He could only watch, frozen in his spot, the woman he had fallen in love with. Her lithe, tall, athletic body, partially hidden in the mist, appeared gold from the reflection of the umber moon; her hair was long and loose, fanning out around her body. It was the most incredible thing he had ever seen. She was the most magnificent creature. For as long as he lived, he would never forget seeing Josephine Brand, dancing nude in the moonlight at the top of the world.

Josephine stopped twirling, appeared to be a little dizzy, and she laughed. The spell was broken. Logan grabbed the blanket out of the tent.

"What are you doing?" he asked her.

Josephine spun around, appeared to be surprised that she wasn't alone anymore. She didn't cover her nakedness, even though she was clearly shivering.

"I'm getting kissed by the moon."

Logan wrapped the blanket over her shoulders. "It's too cold out here for this, Jo. You're going to make yourself sick."

Josephine pulled the blanket tightly around her body. "I woke up so hot. I just wanted to cool off. We can go back now."

She was grateful to be back in his arms. At the time, she hadn't realized how cold her body had become. She hadn't felt it. All she had felt was joy. She felt happy and free and…beautiful. She had danced naked on the Continental Divide. It was a landmark moment. She was changed.

"Come here." Logan opened the sleeping bag for her to crawl inside. "Let me warm you up."

Josephine slipped into the sleeping bag and slipped into Logan's arms. They were facing each other; her breasts, small and pert, brushed against his defined pectoral muscles. She ran her hand over his arm feeling the muscles. She reached for his hand and threaded her fingers together with his. She was used to his hand now. It felt right to hold his hand now.

"My beautiful Josephine." He whispered in the dark. "You are more special than I ever hoped for..."

She pressed her lips to his. She untangled her fingers from his so she could touch his body. The tips of her fingers traced the ridges of his abdomen. Then, her hand moved to his groin. He wasn't aroused—not completely. She wrapped her fingers around his shaft.

"Your hands are freezing..." Logan said.

"Sorry about that." She laughed. "I need you to warm me up again."

"I can do this..." Logan kissed her before he grabbed another condom.

Josephine rolled onto her back and brought him with her. Logan slid inside of her, so slow, so deliberate. He kissed her slowly, sweetly, and he joined their bodies together.

"Josephine...I love you so much."

Those were the last words between them. Logan left her body to guide her onto her stomach. He covered her body with his, one arm under her chest, hand over her breast, and entered her from behind.

"Ah...that feels so good, Logan. Please don't stop..."

Logan had no intention of stopping. He reached beneath her body and rubbed her swollen clit at the same time he loved her with his hard shaft. They rocked together and found a rhythm that felt like ecstasy to both of them.

"I feel you coming, Jo," Logan said in a strained voice. "Come for me…"

And when she did, when she began to shudder in his arms, he couldn't hold his orgasm a moment longer and they reached their climax together.

Breathing heavy from the effort, they collapsed into each other's arms and laughed. They both lay flat on their backs, hands intertwined, the cold air chilling their damp skin.

"I think this may be one of the best nights of my life," Josephine told him. Her feelings were still all over the map, so she couldn't say for sure that she loved him, but she knew that she loved *making love* with him.

Logan looked over at her; he could make out her profile in the dark. He remembered that he had told her that he loved her in the throes of making love. He had meant it, and he didn't want to think about the fact that she hadn't told him that she loved him too. He wanted to tell her that he was having the best time of his life with her, but he held back. Instead, he turned toward her, draped his arm over her stomach, and kissed her goodnight. Right now he needed to sleep; the future would just have to take care of the rest.

Josephine wished that they could stay up on the divide for more than a day. The views were incredible and, at this altitude, she felt like she was closer to God. But her family knew their plan and they needed to pack up and start to head back down the mountain. Riding in the saddle, after a night of lovemaking, was difficult. Her body was tender and sore and it made sitting the saddle really uncomfortable. When they reached the first campsite on their return trip, she got out of the saddle as quick as she could. And she didn't even consider trying to make love with Logan that night. But by the time they reached the last campsite, her body had started to recover and all she could think about was making love. Once they returned to the ranch, they were going to be like bugs in a jar again; privacy and opportunity would be a problem.

They set up the camp and Josephine gathered up some toiletries so she could rinse off in the nearby stream.

"Coming?" she asked Logan.

"Yeah, I definitely need to rinse off."

"Why don't you grab the blanket…" Josephine asked with a mischievous smile, "…and a condom?"

On their trip together, Logan felt that Josephine had experienced her own sexual revolution. She was freer with her body, more assertive about letting him know when she wanted to make love again. And it seemed that the more frequently they made love, the more she wanted it, and even if he was tired, or not really in the mood, he never turned her down. He was going to take every opportunity to love Josephine. Whenever she wanted it, however she wanted it, he was going to be there for her.

Josephine stripped off her clothing, feeling more comfortable with her own body. Before this trip, before Logan, she would have never been naked outdoors. But she discovered that she liked it. It was exciting. Exhilarating.

Logan smiled at her. He loved that she had lost her self-consciousness and felt safe enough with him to stand before him completely exposed. When he took off his pants, Josephine looked down at his arousal with a pleased smile. Just looking at her for a few minutes and he wanted to be with her. No man had ever made her feel more desirable than Logan.

They both waded quickly into the stream. It was so cold that they washed as quickly as they could and then grabbed their towels and ran, laughing, back to the blanket.

"So cold!" Josephine shivered beneath her towel.

Logan dried off quickly, then lay down on the blanket and held out his arms to her. Josephine dropped her towel and unpinned her hair. She had never, in her life, considered making love outdoors, during the day, and she was about to do just that. With a lover's smile on her face, Josephine joined him on the blanket and took him into her mouth. When he was fully aroused, she pushed him back playfully and climbed on top of him. She rode him, rocking her hips back and forth, her long hair brushing his upper thighs.

He watched her pleasure herself with his body, mesmerized by her beauty. She opened her eyes, smiled at him, and then leaned forward so he could take her breast into his mouth. Perhaps it was because they were starting to know each other intimately—the way their bodies could work in unison—but this time was more intense. This time took her to a place that she didn't know existed.

"Oh," she moaned. "Oh, *Logan*…"

"I've got you, baby." He held her tight. "I've got you…"

She wanted him faster, she wanted him harder. She set the frantic pace until they were both panting and shaking and kissing each other breathless as they came together.

Josephine collapsed on top of him, laughing a joyful,

tired laugh. Their bodies still connected, Logan rolled onto his side. He brushed her damp hair away from her face before he happily closed his eyes.

"Logan…" She felt so satisfied in his arms.

"Hmm?"

"I love you, too," she said tentatively at first, and then again with more conviction. "I do love you."

There was a strange feeling at the ranch when they arrived the next day. She was exhausted, but so happy and relaxed. She had laughed more with Logan, explored more, and loved more. The trip shifted her perspective. Everything looked just a little bit different. They took the horses and the mule to the barn to start to unload. At first, she didn't see London. After they had taken the tack off the horses and unpacked the mule, London appeared.

"How was your trip?" the intern asked.

"Amazing!" Josephine hung her bridle on the hook. "You've got to go up there before you head back to the East Coast."

London gave her a placating half smile. It was then that Josephine noticed how swollen and red London's eyes were. She had been crying. Josephine's immediate gut response was that her brother was somehow involved. This was exactly why their father had a long-standing rule that no one on the ranch could get involved with the interns.

"Why don't you guys take off?" London said. "I'll take care of the rest of this stuff."

"Are you sure?" Josephine asked her.

London nodded and then turned her head away from them. Josephine sensed that London wanted to unpack for them so they would leave and she could be alone again.

"Are you coming up to the house?" Josephine asked Logan.

"I hadn't thought about it."

"At least say hi to Mom." She wasn't ready for their time together to be over.

They thanked London and then headed, hand-in-hand, up to the main house. Logan looked down at their linked hands.

"Are you okay with everyone seeing this?"

She was okay with it. Did she know where their relationship was heading? No. She didn't. But she did know that the friendship had turned into an attraction, and on this trip, had grown into love. She loved Logan—as a man, as a friend. And she was "okay" with everyone in her family knowing about it.

They were talking about the trip and laughing when they opened the front door and headed to the kitchen.

"Hey! Anybody home?"

They walked into the kitchen, still holding hands, but when Josephine saw that there was an uninvited guest sitting at the dining table, she stopped smiling and let go of Logan's hand.

"Hi, Josephine." Brice stood up and faced her.

She glanced at Logan quickly. His expression had turned stony as he checked out her ex.

"What are you doing here?" she asked.

"I came to be your date for the wedding." Brice took a tentative step toward her. "Can we go somewhere to talk?"

"You can use the study," her mother said.

Josephine stared at Brice unbelievingly. He shouldn't

be in Montana. He shouldn't be in her family home. He had dumped her, left her dateless to her own twin's wedding. She should hate him for what he did to her. But she didn't. Seeing him now, she realized that she still cared for him. That hadn't been erased. They had been friends first.

She looked at Logan, trying to gauge his reaction.

He gave her a silent nod. She reached out, touched his arm to reassure him, before she addressed Brice.

"We can go to the study."

Brice wanted to hug her. He didn't, but she could see that he wanted to. There was sorrow in his eyes—and regret.

"Where are you going to be?" she asked Logan.

"The cabin. I'll come find you later," he promised.

Brice was in their space now, standing directly in front of them. He was a head and shoulders taller than Logan, which registered in her head, right before she realized that she had been too stunned to introduce them.

"Brice…this is Logan Wolf. Logan…Brice Livingston."

They shook hands. Josephine crossed her arms tightly in front of her. She never imagined that these two men would ever meet.

After an incredible week together, their trip was ending with an awkward twist. Logan headed in one direction and she headed in the other, leading Brice to the study. She waited for Brice to walk through the door, and then she closed the door behind him.

"Welcome to wedding central." She stood by the closed door, arms crossed.

She watched Brice closely. He was such a handsome man—tall and sure of himself. He was the quintessential

California man, with his stylish dusty-blond hair, strong profile, superwhite smile and blue-green eyes. Jordan always said he looked like a Ken doll. For the first time, she saw that maybe he did. Stiff and a bit plastic.

Brice turned to face her, hands in his pockets. "It feels strange to not hug you."

He was fishing for a hug, but she couldn't do it. She just couldn't do it.

"It's strange to see you with someone else," he said. "It's hard."

"I know." Her tone was caustic.

He took a step closer to her. "You look good. Happy."

"Brice…"

"Just hear me out…please…I need to apologize to you."

Josephine frowned, turned her head away, so he couldn't see the pain in her eyes, the tears that were starting to form. She had thought she was over Brice. She thought that she had put all of this pain behind her. And then he showed up, unannounced, with his perfect hair and his perfect clothes and his perfect apology.

"I made a huge mistake, Josie. I know I did. But do we have to throw away five years, Jo? *Five* years?"

A tear slipped down her cheek; Brice held out his handkerchief to her. She shook her head and wiped the tears off on her sleeve.

"Josie…" Brice tried to reach out for her, but she jerked her shoulder away from him.

"No! Shouldn't you be back in California with Caroline?" she asked bitterly.

Brice grimaced. "She's not the person I thought she was." He continued in a lowered voice, "She's not the woman you are, Josephine."

Josephine looked directly into his eyes. It was sincere. His apology was sincere.

He took a step closer to her. "I want us to start over."

"Brice...Logan and I have...been together." How easily those words came out of her mouth.

She saw the pain flash in his eyes. She had thought that causing him pain would make her feel better. It hadn't. Brice's eyes became hooded; his shoulders stiffened. "We both made mistakes..."

She pointed to her chest; she raised her voice to him, something out of character for her. "*I* didn't do this. *You* did this, Brice. This is all on you."

He held up his hands in surrender. "No, you're right. You're right. It was me. It was all me. But come on, Jo, I love you. We can start over...all you have to do is say yes."

Chapter Fifteen

Logan didn't come to find her. Instead, she found him inside of the chapel, working. The wedding was only a couple of days away and he had said on their trip up to the divide that he was anxious to get it ready for Ian and Jordan.

"You said you were going to come and find me." She didn't want to engage in small talk with this man. After what they had shared on the mountain, it seemed like an insult to both of them.

Logan drilled a screw into one of the broken pews before he stood up and faced her. "I wanted to give you some space."

"You're really big on that, I know." Why was she taking this out on him?

Logan stared at her, and then with a small shake of his head, he knelt down again.

"Sorry..." Josephine sat down heavily in a nearby pew, leaned forward and rested her elbows on her legs. She felt weary and defeated. She had moved on during her trip with Logan, and then she came home, only to be slammed right back into her past with Brice.

"He wants to get back together."

Logan continued to work while they talked. "I know. A man doesn't come all this way without a motive in mind."

She looked down at her entwined fingers. He was right and they both knew it. But for once, she wished that Logan would get mad, ask questions, or demand answers. Why did he always have to be so calm and introspective?

"Brice is staying for the wedding."

When she told him that, she saw a small chink in his armor. His eyebrows drawn together, he stopped his work to look her way. "I'm surprised to hear that."

"I know...I know. So was I, frankly, especially with how my family has always felt about him. But he's an invited guest. Jordan never took him off the guest list— and he came all of this way. You've heard of Southern hospitality...we kind of have our own version of that in Montana." When he didn't respond, she added, "But he's not staying at the ranch, and he's not going as my date, Logan. I told him that we've been together..."

Logan's head dropped down and he breathed in deeply, like he was trying to gather his thoughts before he answered. His head still dropped, he said to her quietly, "I know you didn't invite him here, Josephine. That's not what's bothering me." He stood up, drill still in his hand. "What's bothering me is that you didn't tell him to leave..."

* * *

Even though it felt like her private world was a mess, she didn't really have time to fix it, because life on the ranch had kicked into high gear. The list of last-minute preparations for the wedding had tripled, along with her mother's anxiety level. Everyone was busy, everyone was in a rush, and Josephine needed to put aside her problems in her relationship with Logan to focus exclusively on helping her sister prepare for one of the most important days of her life. Brice hadn't left Montana, which was a surprise to her. She hadn't promised him anything, she hadn't encouraged him to stay, but he was determined to attend the wedding anyway. The only positive she could find about him being nearby, contrite and willing to talk, was that she could ask him questions about what really happened between them. She could ask him questions about what had happened between him and the woman that was so appealing to him that he had thrown away their relationship and their future plans. But the answers he gave her always left her with a bigger question mark. He wanted her back, but she could never figure out exactly *why*.

"Oh, my goodness, Jordy...I've never seen you look more beautiful."

It was the morning of the wedding. The rehearsal dinner had gone off without a hitch, and now the day they had all been waiting for, the day that they had all been working toward, was here.

Jordan, who rarely cried, started to tear up when she saw herself for the first time, fully dressed in her wedding ensemble.

"Wait, don't cry. You'll mess up your makeup!" Josephine rushed to grab a handkerchief out of her purse to hand to her sister. "Here, but blot, Jordan. Don't wipe, blot."

Jordan blew her nose into the handkerchief loudly completely bypassing the "blotting" instructions. Her sister looked at the handkerchief, saw the initials *BL* embroidered in fancy scroll on the corner.

"Ugh." Her twin wrinkled up her nose, balled up the handkerchief in her fist and then threw it in a small garbage can.

"Jordy...that wasn't mine!"

"Don't you *dare* fish that out of the trash, Jo. That's where it belongs," her sister said. "Why do you have it anyway?"

"I sneezed earlier, and he gave it to me. My gosh, Jordy, don't look so disappointed. I borrowed a handkerchief. I didn't have sex with him in one of the pews."

Jordan hugged her then. Tightly and for a long time. "I just want you to find what I have with Ian, Jo. You deserve that. I've never loved anyone like I love that man. I haven't had a moment of doubt about marrying him since the day he put this ring on my finger."

"I want that, too."

Still holding on to her arms, Jordan pulled back so she could look into her eyes. "I don't know if you could have that with Logan. I don't. But you're my sister and my loyalty is always going to be with you. But Logan's my friend, too, Jo, and Ian says he's really hurting over this whole Brice thing. Ian told me that, until you, Logan hasn't been serious about anyone since his divorce."

Logan had told her once before that he had been married, but she had never pried.

"Do you know anything about his ex?"

"Yeah...she was his childhood sweetheart. I think

they were in a band together in high school or something like that."

Jordan adjusted her veil, which was her something borrowed. It was the veil that her mom had worn when she married their dad. "Is this right?"

Josephine helped her sister straighten the veil. She had known Logan was married before, but somehow it felt like she was hearing this information for the first time.

"Anyway...she did a real number on him, from what Ian tells me. She backed up a U-Haul while he was at work and cleaned out their apartment. She took everything. He got home and found her gone, along with everything they owned. Horrible, right?"

Josephine nodded. It was horrible.

Barbara Brand, followed by a posse of wedding planners, burst into the room and that stopped her from asking her sister another question about Logan's wife. Ex-wife.

"We're almost ready to start, my beauties!" Barbara's voice was higher and tenser than usual. "Hurry, hurry! You've got to get into place!"

"Is this straight?" Ian asked Logan to check his bow tie. The last time he'd had a tux on was the night he proposed to Jordan.

Ian stood still while Logan adjusted his tie. "Now it's straight."

Ian and Logan stood quietly together for a moment. There was a lot of commotion and voices on the other side of the door, but in their small room in the church, it was calm. Shadow, who was awaiting his next command, was sitting at attention by the door.

"Thank you for being my best man, Logan," Ian said to him.

"I felt really honored that I was the person you thought of when Dylan couldn't make it."

Ian gave a slight nod of his head. Then he said, in a lowered voice, "I'm sorry that Brice is here, Logan. If it had been up to me, he wouldn't have stepped inside the church today."

"It is what it is…" Logan tried to sound casual about it. But he hated the fact that Brice was at the wedding. He hated the strain Josephine's ex had already caused in his fragile relationship with the woman he loved.

A knock on the door stopped the conversation. They were ready for them to take their place in the church.

"You ready?" Logan asked his friend.

"I've been ready." Ian took hold of the handle on the special harness Shadow was wearing. "There're only two things I've ever been sure about in my life—being a photographer and marrying Jordan."

Logan and Ian took their place at the front of the church, and then waited for the rest of the wedding party to join them. Logan locked eyes with Brice, who was sitting next to Luke, Josephine's older brother, and his wife, Sophia, in the front pews reserved for the Brand family.

There was a challenge in Brice's look. Logan recognized it and knew that he hadn't abandoned the idea of reuniting with Josephine. The man was wealthy, privileged, entitled, and used to getting everything he wanted when he wanted it. He was definitely a problem.

The wedding procession started and Josephine, in a floor-length royal purple gown, started to walk slowly up the aisle toward them. He had never seen her look this lovely. She would, for the remainder of his life, be the most beautiful woman he had ever seen. Being separated from her like this since they returned from the divide felt like a third-degree burn all over his body that no one else could see. He was in pain, pure and simple, and he had sworn, after Alicia, that he was never going to put himself in a position to let it happen again. That pact he had made with himself was broken when he fell in love with Josephine Brand.

Josephine took her place at the front of the church. She hadn't been able to take her eyes off of Logan in his tuxedo. So strong and handsome—and this time, when she compared him to Brice, it was her ex who came up short. When the wedding march started, all of Josephine's attention was on her twin. Jordan, a statuesque and modern bride, stood next to their father. Hank looked more proud at that moment with her sister on his arm than she had ever seen him look before. As she walked down the aisle toward her waiting fiancé, her elegant twin sister seemed to be so much more mature since she met Ian Sterling. He was a good balance for her; he kept her grounded. Jordan had met her perfect match in Ian, and Josephine wondered, as the two of them began to exchange their vows, if she hadn't met her own perfect match in Logan. Now, when she looked at him, as he stood just behind Ian, all she could think about was how his lips felt on her skin, on her mouth, when he kissed her.

After the ceremony, a limousine took Ian and his new bride to the reception. A family friend, who owned a multimillion dollar spread just outside of Helena, had offered to hold the reception at his ranch house. This wasn't just any old ranch house; it was a Montana mansion in its own right. Tents had been erected outside and there was a large outdoor area, covered in twinkling lights and fragrant flowers, large enough for the band and for dancing. Tables were set up in the tent for dining and they all gathered there to eat before the dancing began. She was seated at a long table at the front of the tent that was reserved for the bride, groom, and wedding party. According to the seating arrangement, she was to sit next to Logan.

"Let me get that for you." Logan moved behind her and pulled out her chair for her.

"Thank you."

He took the seat next to her, and it occurred to her that this was the first time they were sitting down together since they returned from their camping trip. She couldn't stop looking at his hands—those hands had touched all of her body. Even though they hadn't made love since their return, she could still remember the feel of his lips on hers, and the weight of his body between her thighs, how amazing it felt to have his body completely fill hers.

"That's quite a dress." Logan's statement brought her out of her own head and back into reality. That was more than he had said to her in several days.

She looked down at her gown. "I didn't want to get it. I thought it might come close to upstaging the bride, it's so beautiful. But Jordan insisted. She wanted me to look…beautiful."

"She succeeded."

"Thank you. You look handsome." She returned the compliment. "I've never seen you like this before."

"It's far and few between, trust me," he said. "I'm not normally a tuxedo kind of guy."

After the meal, and after the toasts, most of the guests moved out to the open dance floor where there was a free liquor bar and a live band. Logan had already left the table, so she headed outside. Brice followed her.

"As always, you look incredible tonight, Josie."

Josephine picked a spot away with an unimpeded view of the band. "Thank you.

Brice knew how to wear a tuxedo—that was his comfort zone, his realm of experience, and he presented a handsome, hard-to-resist exterior. But he was wearing the same tuxedo he was wearing in the picture when she first saw him with another woman. She couldn't bring herself to return his compliment.

"Did I ever tell you that I'm not really fond of the nickname Josie?" She looked up into his face, a face she had admired thousands of times before.

"What? No. You never have. Why would you let me call you by a nickname for all these years that you didn't like?"

"That…" Josephine responded, "…is a very good question."

Brice repositioned himself so he was in front of her, blocking the view of the band.

"Josephine, I came all this way to prove to you that I'm sincere. I made a mistake, and I want to make it up to you. I want to make things right between us. You're one of my best friends, Josie…Josephine…I don't want to lose that."

Logan returned from the men's room to discover that Josephine had left the table. When he didn't find her in the dining area, he looked for her outside. He spotted her, apparently in a deep conversation with Brice. Brice was standing very close to her with his head was bent down toward her. They weren't touching, but their natural comfort from years of being a couple showed. Logan almost turned and walked away. He almost did. But then it dawned on him. Perhaps Josephine had been waiting for him to fight for her. Perhaps Josephine needed him to show up, be present, and claim her for his own. He went to the stage and put in a request for a song. Then he walked directly across the dance floor to Josephine.

"Excuse me…" he interrupted. "I'd like to have this dance, Josephine."

Josephine glanced quickly between Brice and Logan, two men whom she loved, and two men who loved her. She was standing at an unspoken crossroad, and all three of them knew it.

"I'd like that. Thank you." Josephine didn't look at Brice when she took Logan's offered hand.

"We'll talk later," she told Brice.

Logan took her into his arms, and they began to sway together to Eric Clapton's "Wonderful Tonight."

"I love this song."

"I requested it for you," he told her.

Josephine smiled at him. With her heels on, she was a little bit taller than he was. She thought it would bother her, but it didn't. He was such a masculine gentleman that his lack of height seemed insignificant.

When Logan heard a certain part of the song, he pulled her closer to him so he could sing a line or two in her ear.

When he sang to her, all of the moments she had shared with him flashed through her mind. His voice, so rich and sexy, made her want to more than just dance with him. And she knew that he felt exactly the same way. Their bodies, whenever they were close, were a perfect fit.

Logan felt a tap on his shoulder.

"I'd like to cut in…" Brice had left the side of the dance floor and was standing directly next to them.

Logan slowed a bit, but didn't stop dancing, and he didn't let go of her. Her heart seized for a second, because there was something definitely brewing between these two alpha males.

"Not this time," Logan told him and then spun her away from Brice.

Brice turned red in the face and he grabbed Logan's arm. In an instant, Logan's officer training kicked in and the next thing she knew, Brice was taken down to the ground in his custom tuxedo.

Logan stepped back, prepared for a next attack. Brice was quickly on his feet; he'd boxed in college and she could see his stance. He was going to punch Logan.

"Brice! *Don't!* He's a cop!" she tried to warn her ex. Assault on a law enforcement officer could derail Brice's career.

Brice ignored her warning, balled up his fist, and lunged at Logan. Logan ducked to the side, deflected the punch, grabbed Brice's wrist and twisted it around so his arm was behind his back and Logan had complete control of him. Logan took him down again, quickly lowered him to the ground, but this time, he wasn't gentle. He slammed Brice down, so he would *stay* down.

Instinctively, after years of being with Brice, she ran to his side and knelt down beside him to make sure he wasn't seriously hurt.

Logan stared at her with a look that could only be described as wounded and betrayed.

"Stay down," he told Brice, before he turned around and disappeared into the crowd that had gathered around them.

After she made sure Brice was okay, she searched for Logan, only to find out that he had decided to leave the reception early and return to the ranch. She wouldn't leave her twin's wedding reception to chase after him, but she did do the one thing that she should have done right from the start: she told Brice to leave.

The morning after the wedding, the ranch seemed so quiet compared to the pre-wedding chaos. Ian and Jordan had already taken off to start their honeymoon in the Caribbean island of Curaçao, where they had first fallen in love. And even her brother Luke and his wife, Sophia, had left for the airport because they both needed to get back to Boston for work and to take care of their three kids. Josephine had awakened with one thing on her mind: Logan. She skipped her usual stop, the kitchen, and headed straight to Tyler's cabin.

At the same time she was opening the front door, Tyler was coming out of his bedroom. They met in the kitchen and Tyler poured a cup of coffee for himself.

"He's up at the chapel," her brother said. "Coffee?"

"No, thanks." Josephine noticed several packed bags piled up just outside of the guest bedroom. She stared at them for several seconds, feeling sick to her stomach.

"Are those Logan's?"

Tyler nodded before he took a sip of his coffee.

Logan was leaving. She swallowed hard several times before she asked, "Did he say where he's going?"

"No. And I didn't think to ask," her brother said. "I take it you didn't know he was leaving."

Josephine shook her head. "I really screwed up with him, Tyler," she admitted.

"I doubt it's anything fatal. I think he's a really good guy. I'd go talk to him if I were you," her brother advised.

"Yeah…" She slid off the bench. "I guess I will."

Before she dealt with her own relationship issues, she knew she needed to talk to Tyler about his. "I've been so caught up with my own drama that I almost forgot to ask you…what exactly did you do to her?"

Tyler put his coffee cup down on the counter. "Who are you talking about?"

"London."

She saw it, the flash of pain on his face when she mentioned the intern's name. "She looked like she was crying the other day."

"She was?" Tyler seemed caught off-guard by her comment. "Did she tell you why?"

"No, but I do know you're involved with her, Tyler. Don't ask me how I know—I just do, okay? So what did you do?"

Tyler looked away from her, shook his head in thought, before he turned his face back toward her.

"She's pregnant."

"Oh…" Josephine stared at him, shocked. "Tyler, that's not good."

Tyler's face took on a stony appearance. "London would agree with you on that point."

"And you don't?" she asked him. Out of all of the siblings, Tyler had always been the slowest to want to grow up. He had always been serious about ranching, but he'd always sworn that he'd never settle down, get married, and have a family.

"No. Actually, I don't." Tyler dumped the rest of his coffee into the sink. "I'm in love with her, Jo. I want to marry her and raise our child here on the ranch. But until we've figured this out, I'd appreciate it if you'd keep this to yourself."

Josephine hugged her brother and promised to keep the secret.

"I'm having a hard enough time trying to fix my own life," she said. "Trust me, I don't think I'm in a good position to give relationship advice."

Chapter Sixteen

Josephine rehearsed what she wanted to say to Logan on her way up the hill to the chapel. She knew that there were so many things that she needed to say…wanted to say…that they were all jumbled together. Even though her thoughts were jumbled, the main purpose of this encounter with Logan was perfectly clear: she owed him an apology. A big one.

Once she reached the chapel's door, she paused to collect her thoughts. Josephine put her hand on her churning stomach as she reached for the door handle. She felt nervous and upset mixed with a gnawing sense of foreboding. What if Logan didn't accept her apology? What then?

Josephine slowly pushed the heavy wooden door open. The inside of the chapel still needed a lot of TLC, but Logan and the rest of the crew had done a remarkable job getting the outside of the chapel picture-perfect for the wedding.

She closed the door quietly behind her and walked down the aisle. Logan, her Logan, was leaning against the podium, writing.

"Hi…" She stopped just on the other side of the podium.

"Hey," Logan said before he clenched the pencil between his teeth, grabbed a measuring tape, and walked to the other side of the chapel.

"I stopped by Tyler's. You're leaving."

Logan measured one of the thick stained-glass windows, before he returned to the podium to write down the window's dimensions into a notebook.

"That's right." Logan moved on to the next window and started to measure it.

Josephine crossed her arms defensively in front of her body. He couldn't…wouldn't…even look at her.

"Were you even planning on saying goodbye?" she asked caustically. "Or were you just going to up and leave?"

Logan let the measuring tape snap back into place. He turned around and met her eyes for the first time. "I wouldn't do that to you."

"No, I know." She contemplated the ground. "That's not your style."

This wasn't going at all like she had rehearsed. Instead of cleaning up the mess as she had intended, she was making it bigger.

"Could you just…stop…for a minute." Josephine put her hand on Logan's arm.

Logan looked at her hand on his arm. "I'm leaving today, Josephine. Let me finish what I started here."

"But that's what I'm trying to do…finish what we started."

With a frustrated sigh, Logan finally looked up at her.

"Look…I'm not up for any more drama, okay? I knew that you were fresh off a breakup, Jo. And I knew you needed more time, but I fell in love with you and I didn't want to wait. That was my mistake, not yours. I knew better. "

"I fell in love with you, too," Josephine told him quickly.

"Maybe you did. Maybe you didn't. Either way, I think we need to step back and give each other some space to think."

Josephine shook her head. "No. We don't need space. Quit giving me so much space! Why won't you fight for me?"

She saw a rare flash of anger in Logan's black, enigmatic eyes. She'd take the anger—it was better than the cold shoulder he'd been giving her ever since she had arrived.

"Fight for you?" he asked incredulously.

"Yes." She held his gaze. "If you want me, I'm right here. Fight for me."

Instead of talking, he acted. Logan grabbed her, pulled her into his arms, and kissed her hard on the mouth. When he kissed her this time, he was laying claim to her. His fingers, such strong, rough, calloused fingers, held her face while he deepened the kiss.

Logan broke the kiss, tilted his head back, and studied her through narrowed eyes.

"Where's the pretty boy?" he asked.

Josephine leaned into Logan's body, wanting more of his kisses. "I sent him packing…"

"About damn time," he said before he kissed her again.

Standing inside the rustic chapel, in the arms of the man she loved, Josephine truly knew, for the first time, exactly what she wanted.

"Logan?"

"Hmm?" Logan was nibbling on the side of her neck, breathing in the scent of her freshly washed skin.

"Will you marry me?"

The nibbling stopped. Logan leaned back, surprised, and stared at her.

"What did you just say?"

Josephine wiggled out of his arms. "You heard me. Will you?"

Logan rubbed his forehead and gave a little shake of his head.

"You're proposing to me?"

Her arms were crossed again. She gave a quick, silent nod.

"I'm not sure what I'm supposed to say here."

Her face felt hot—it had to be red and splotchy from the rush of embarrassment she was feeling.

"And now I feel really stupid..."

Josephine tried to escape, but Logan caught her hand and kept her from walking away from him.

"Wait a minute, you can't just spring a question like that on me and then walk away. Jesus, Jo, you gotta give a guy a chance to process..."

"No. I waited for five years while Brice processed. I love you and I want to be your wife. What do you want?"

"I want to be your husband." Plain, simple, truthful.

"Then it's a yes," she said with a smile.

Logan kissed her in that slow, gentle way of his. "It's a yes. But…I get to propose."

"But I just proposed."

"Jo, we aren't going to get married until I propose. That's my deal." Logan grabbed the notebook off the podium and then he grabbed her hand. "I get to pick the time and the place for our official engagement."

"But we're engaged now, right? I asked and you answered."

Logan opened the door for her.

"You're a strong, determined woman, Jo…and I love that about you. But, sometimes, you're just going to have to let me be the man."

"Where do you think you left it?" Josephine asked her twin.

"I don't know. But we can't get in without that reservation card."

It was their birthday and Jordan, who wasn't into pampering, had, as a present to her, made them both reservations at a ritzy San Diego spa. But, when she met her sister in the lobby of their downtown penthouse, Jordan realized that she didn't have the reservation card in her wallet.

"Let's just go back up and look for it." Jordan waved at the lobby attendant and they got into the elevator to go forty-four floors back up to the penthouse.

"We're going to be late." Josephine followed her sister into the elevator.

"No, it's just right around the corner. We'll be fine."

Once inside the penthouse, they climbed up the stairs to the second story of the condo. Josephine was always struck by the views. The condo offered spectacular 180-degree views of the San Diego harbor.

"You check out on the balcony and I'll check my other purse," Jordan told her.

"Why would it be out on the balcony?"

"Oh, my *God*, Jo! You're so argumentative! I was out there yesterday and I think I may have left it on the table. Just *go*!"

Josephine opened the balcony door, and the first thing she saw was Logan Wolf standing by an enormous wrapped box, holding a sunflower. The balcony was covered with sunflowers. Everywhere she looked, she saw sunflowers.

"Happy birthday, Jo," Logan said.

Josephine took a step out onto the balcony, her eyes flitting from one huge sunflower arrangement to the next. "I thought you had to work…"

"I may have misled you a little there." Logan walked over to her, handed her the single sunflower, then he kissed her.

"All right, you two. Have a good time." Jordan appeared in the doorway.

"Where are you going?"

"Ian's flying me to New York for the weekend. The place is all yours." Jordan gave her sister a hug. "Happy birthday, Jo."

"Happy birthday, Jordy." She kissed her twin on the cheek. "You still owe me a spa day."

Jordan laughed, waved, and then shut the balcony door behind her. When they were alone, Jo pointed to the box.

"Is that for me?"

"I wrapped it myself."

Josephine laid the sunflower on the table and examined the box. "You're not an accomplished wrapper, are you?"

Logan laughed with good nature. "Just open the box."

Josephine pulled the giant white bow off the top of the box and stuck it on top of her head. She ripped the paper off the box and pried it open. Inside the giant box, was another, slightly smaller, wrapped box.

"Really?" she asked him. "That's how you're going to roll?"

Logan looked pleased with himself. "That's how I'm going to roll. Start unwrapping."

Box after wrapped box, Josephine ripped off the paper, only to discover a box within a box. Finally, she found what had to be the last box.

She raised her eyebrows playfully at Logan and shook the box. "This has to be the last one, right?"

"I don't know. Open it and see."

She quickly ripped the wrapping off the box and found a little black velvet jewelry box inside. She stared at the box for a second or two, her heart beating faster and faster with nervous anticipation of what might be inside of the box.

"Here, let me help you with that." Logan took it from her hands, took the jewelry box out, and put the empty one on the table.

Logan opened the box and showed her the contents.

She had expected to see a ring. Instead, she saw a folded piece of paper. Confused and curious, Josephine unfolded the piece of paper and realized that she was unfolding the form that San Diego police officers used to write tickets. In Logan's handwriting, in bold letters written across the ticket, there was a message for her: *Will you marry me?*

Logan bent down on one knee in front of her with a diamond ring in his hand. "Will you marry me, Jo?"

Josephine nodded her head quickly. "Of course I will."

Logan slipped the ring on her finger. It was a brilliant cut stone set in platinum. It wasn't a large stone, but it was nearly a hundred years old and in an antique setting. Just like Logan was the perfect man for her, the ring he had chosen was a perfect fit.

"I love you." Josephine hugged him tightly, kissed him sweetly. She had been waiting for this day for such a long time. "We're officially engaged!"

"I don't know how I got so lucky, but I'm glad that you do love me." He held her face in his hands and kissed her back. "I'm so glad that you do."

He had planned for them to stay in the condo guest room, but Josephine had insisted that they spend the night at his modest, sparsely furnished condo in Chula Vista.

Logan unlocked the front door, turned on the light switch at the door, and then let Josephine enter in front of him. He always felt a little embarrassed when Josephine came over. He knew she was used to much fancier digs, but this was the best he could do on his salary.

"We'll find a new place that works for both of us." Logan shut the door behind him. "I'm not expecting you to live in this dump once we're married."

"I don't think this is a dump." Josephine slipped off her strappy heels. "I like your place."

"Why?"

Josephine walked over to him, barefoot. She put her

arms around her fiancé's waist. "Because it's yours...I love it here because I love you."

"It might not get much better than this on a cop's salary, Jo. Are you sure you can handle that?"

"Are you trying to back out of our engagement already?" she teased him.

He still had his hands in his pockets. His body posture was stiff and a little bit defensive. "I just want to make sure this is the life you really want."

"I want a life with you, whatever that brings. Okay?" Josephine grabbed his hand and led him to the small efficiency kitchen to find something in which to put her sunflower. "I'm going to be graduating soon, so don't forget, I'll have an income, too. Of course, I want to be a public defender and do a lot of pro bono work, so if you were thinking you were getting a high-priced attorney, you're barking up the wrong tree."

Josephine filled a large plastic cup full of water and stuck her sunflower in it.

Logan came up behind her, wrapped his arms around her waist, and kissed the back of her neck.

"Hmm..." She closed her eyes. "I've missed you."

At the end of summer, they had flown back to California together on Ian's private jet. Logan returned to San Diego and she went back to Berkeley to finish her degree. Their relationship had to be long-distance and sometimes they only saw each other a couple times a month. But they had spent hours getting to know each other by phone and Josephine believed that their forced distance had somehow made them stronger as a couple.

"I've missed you."

Josephine turned in his arms so she could kiss him on the mouth. She loved to kiss this man; she had to believe that she always would. There was something about the firmness of his lips; there was something about the natural scent of his skin and his taste that drove her senses crazy.

"Why don't we close the curtains?" she asked him.

Logan smiled at her with his eyes. He knew exactly what she wanted. She wanted to skip dinner and dessert and head straight to bed. They both closed the curtains to shut out the world temporarily. Josephine grabbed two glasses and a bottle of wine from the fridge before she headed to Logan's bedroom.

She pulled her short shift dress over her head and hung it up on one of the empty wire hangers in the closet. Next her bra and panties came off, her hair was let down, and the only thing she was wearing was her new engagement ring.

"You are too beautiful for words." Logan was watching her from the bedroom door.

"Don't you have too many clothes on?" she asked him, completely comfortable in her own skin before her future husband.

Logan undressed and tossed his clothing on the dresser. Then, he joined her, half-aroused, in his bed.

Josephine handed him a glass of wine and then held out her glass for a toast.

"Happy birthday, sweetheart," Logan said.

"Thank you. Logan, this is the best birthday I've ever had. I can't wait to be your wife."

They touched glasses and then Josephine took a sip of the red wine. She immediately made a disgusted face and looked at the wine in her glass.

"*Yuck!* What is this?" She put down her glass and grabbed the bottle.

"I don't know." Logan took another large sip of the wine. "It's not all that bad, is it?"

"No, don't drink that." Josephine took his glass out of his hand. "It's rancid."

"Hey, I wasn't done with that yet."

"Yes, you were," she told him. "Besides, you have some work to do, Lieutenant."

"Is that so?" Logan's eyes traveled from her eyes to her lips to her small, perky breasts. He reached out and encircled one nipple with his finger and he smiled, pleased, when it hardened and puckered beneath his light touch.

"Yes…" Josephine lay down beside him, offering herself to the man she loved. "That's so."

Logan skipped the foreplay and gave her exactly what she had been craving, a body-to-body connection. He slipped inside of her, filling her so completely. She liked it when Logan took control in the bedroom; she liked it when he manhandled her. Everything he did, everything he showed her, was pure pleasure.

Logan hooked his arm under her long leg and bent it toward her chest so he could go deeper within her. Josephine gasped, her head tossed back at the new sensation.

"Do you like that?" He was watching every expression that passed over her face.

"Yes…" she said urgently, not wanting him to stop what he was doing. "That…feels…so good…"

He loved her like that, stroking her, massaging her, filling her deeper and deeper, harder and harder, until he felt her grow completely still beneath him. He opened his eyes, and saw a look of unadulterated joy on her face.

Then she cried out and he felt a rush of wetness on his shaft. Wave after wave, her orgasm didn't stop. She was wild beneath him, drenching him with her love. Logan held her hands over her head and surged into her; the more she soaked him, the more excited he became.

"Josephine…Josephine….*Josephine*…"

She watched him, fascinated at the expression on his handsome face when he came. She arched her back and took him deeper inside of her. They were so close, so connected, that she felt his body pulse inside of her just before he cried out her name three times.

Logan collapsed on top of her and she hugged him close to her. After a minute, he lifted his head and looked at her in amazement. They both laughed.

"What *was* that?" he asked her.

Satiated, Josephine laughed. "You hit my G-spot."

He looked at her in total amazement. That orgasm that they had experienced together, that they had created together, was beyond his experience.

He kissed her on the lips. "And here I always thought that was a mythical creature like a unicorn."

She laughed again. "Me, too!"

Logan rolled onto his side, still holding her hand, and lay flat on his back, one hand behind his head, on top of the sheets. Josephine scooted closer to him, pulled the sheet over her hips, and rested her head on his shoulder. She placed her hand, her left hand with a new engagement ring on her fourth finger, over his heart.

"It's still your birthday, Jo. What do you want to do? I'll take you anywhere you want to go."

Josephine flipped onto her stomach, rested her hand and chin on his chest so she could get a better look at his handsome face.

"I don't need to go anywhere. I'm exactly where I want to be. With you."

Logan's smile started in his dark, enigmatic eyes and then reached his beautifully shaped lips. He rolled her over onto her back so he could look down into wide blue eyes.

"Every day I love you more deeply than the day before, Josephine. I don't know how a guy like me managed to get a woman like you, but I'm the luckiest man I know."

Josephine put her hands on either side of his handsome face and smiled up at him. She knew now what true love felt like. She knew now what it was to feel layers upon layers of happiness and joy. When she had least expected it, when she hadn't even been looking, there he was, finally…her perfect match.

* * * * *

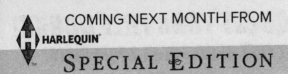
Available May 19, 2015

#2407 FORTUNE'S JUNE BRIDE
The Fortunes of Texas: Cowboy Country • by Allison Leigh
Galen Fortune Jones isn't the marrying kind...until he's roped into playing groom at the new Cowboy Country theme park in Horseback Hollow, Texas. His "bride," beautiful Aurora McElroy, piques his interest, especially when she needs a real-life fake husband. This one cowboy may have just met his match!

#2408 THE PRINCESS AND THE SINGLE DAD
Royal Babies • by Leanne Banks
Princess Sasha of Sergenia fled her dangerous home country for the principality of Chantaine. There, she assumes another identity: nanny to handsome construction specialist Gavin Sinclair's two adorable children. As the princess falls hard for the proud papa, can she form a royal family of her very own?

#2409 HER RED-CARPET ROMANCE
Matchmaking Mamas • by Marie Ferrarella
Film producer Lukas Spader needs to get his work life in order, so he hires professional organizer Yohanna Andrzejewski. She's temptingly beautiful, but Lukas must keep his eyes on his job, not his stunning new employee. As Cupid's arrow strikes them both, though, Yohanna might just fix her sexy boss's life into a happily-ever-after!

#2410 THE INSTANT FAMILY MAN
The Barlow Brothers • by Shirley Jump
Luke Barlow is happily living the single life in Stone Gap, North Carolina—until his ex's gorgeous little sister, Peyton Reynolds, shows up. She announces Luke is now the caretaker for a four-year-old daughter he never knew about. Determined to be a good dad, Luke tries to create a home for little Maddy and her aunt, one that might just be for forever...

#2411 DYLAN'S DADDY DILEMMA
The Colorado Fosters • by Tracy Madison
Chelsea Bell needs help—fast. The single mom has landed in Steamboat Springs, Colorado, and is out of money. So when dashing Dylan Foster offers her and her son, Henry, a place to stay, Chelsea's floored. Why would a complete stranger offer her help, let alone bond with her little boy? This is just the first surprise in store for one unexpected family.

#2412 FALLING FOR THE MOM-TO-BE
Home in Heartlandia • by Lynne Marshall
Ever since his wife passed away, Leif Andersen has had no time for love. Enter Marta Hoyas, a beautiful—and *pregnant!*—artist who's in town to paint a local mural. She's also living in Leif's house while she does so. The last thing Marta wants is to fall for someone who couldn't be a father to her unborn child, but Leif might just be the perfect dad-to-be.

HSECNM0515

REQUEST YOUR FREE BOOKS!
2 FREE NOVELS PLUS 2 FREE GIFTS!

H HARLEQUIN®

SPECIAL EDITION

Life, Love & Family

YES! Please send me 2 FREE Harlequin® Special Edition novels and my 2 FREE gifts (gifts are worth about $10). After receiving them, if I don't wish to receive any more books, I can return the shipping statement marked "cancel." If I don't cancel, I will receive 6 brand-new novels every month and be billed just $4.74 per book in the U.S. or $5.49 per book in Canada. That's a savings of at least 12% off the cover price! It's quite a bargain! Shipping and handling is just 50¢ per book in the U.S. and 75¢ per book in Canada.* I understand that accepting the 2 free books and gifts places me under no obligation to buy anything. I can always return a shipment and cancel at any time. Even if I never buy another book, the two free books and gifts are mine to keep forever.

235/335 HDN GH3Z

Name _____ (PLEASE PRINT) _____

Address _____ Apt. # _____

City _____ State/Prov. _____ Zip/Postal Code _____

Signature (if under 18, a parent or guardian must sign) _____

Mail to the Reader Service:
IN U.S.A.: P.O. Box 1867, Buffalo, NY 14240-1867
IN CANADA: P.O. Box 609, Fort Erie, Ontario L2A 5X3

Want to try two free books from another line?
Call 1-800-873-8635 or visit www.ReaderService.com.

* Terms and prices subject to change without notice. Prices do not include applicable taxes. Sales tax applicable in N.Y. Canadian residents will be charged applicable taxes. Offer not valid in Quebec. This offer is limited to one order per household. Not valid for current subscribers to Harlequin Special Edition books. All orders subject to credit approval. Credit or debit balances in a customer's account(s) may be offset by any other outstanding balance owed by or to the customer. Please allow 4 to 6 weeks for delivery. Offer available while quantities last.

Your Privacy—The Reader Service is committed to protecting your privacy. Our Privacy Policy is available online at www.ReaderService.com or upon request from the Reader Service.

We make a portion of our mailing list available to reputable third parties that offer products we believe may interest you. If you prefer that we not exchange your name with third parties, or if you wish to clarify or modify your communication preferences, please visit us at www.ReaderService.com/consumerchoice or write to us at Reader Service Preference Service, P.O. Box 9062, Buffalo, NY 14240-9062. Include your complete name and address.

HSE15

Galen tucked the "deed" into his shirt and nudged along
his horse, Blaze, with a squeeze of his knees. He set his
white hat more firmly on his head so it wouldn't go blowing off when they made their mad dash down Main. "But
I'm definitely not looking for a career change. Ranching's
in my blood. Only thing I ever wanted to do. Amusing as
this might be for now, I'll be happy as hell to hand over
Rusty's hat to whoever they get to replace Joey." He took
in the other riders as well as Cabot and gathered his reins.
"Y'all ready?"

They nodded, and as one, they set off in a thunder of
horse hooves.

Eleven minutes later on the dot, he was pulling Aurora
into his arms after "knocking" Frank off his feet, saying "I do" to Harlan's Preacher Man and bending Aurora
low over his arm while the audience—always larger on a

Saturday—clapped and hooted.

Unfortunately for Galen, the longer he'd gone without Rusty actually kissing Lila, the more he couldn't stop thinking about it as he pressed his cheek against Aurora's, her head tucked down in his chest.

"Big crowd," he whispered. The mikes were dead and he held her a little longer than usual. Because of the lengthy applause they were getting, of course.

"Too big," she whispered back. "You going to let me up anytime soon?"

He immediately straightened, and she smiled broadly at the crowd, waving her hand as she tucked her hand through his arm and they strolled offstage.

But he could see through the smile to the frustration brewing in her blue eyes.

He waited until they were well away from the stage. "Sorry about that."

"About what?" She impatiently pushed her veil behind her back and kept looking over her shoulder as they strode through the side street. She was damn near jogging, and the beads hanging from her dress were bouncing.

"Holding the…uh…the…uh…" He yanked his string tie loose, feeling like an idiot. "You know. The embrace."

She gave him a distracted look. "What about it?"

"Holding it so long."

Don't miss
FORTUNE'S JUNE BRIDE
by Allison Leigh,
available June 2015 wherever
Harlequin® *Special Edition books and ebooks are sold.*

www.Harlequin.com

Love the Harlequin book you just read?

Your opinion matters.

Review this book on your favorite book site, review site, blog or your own social media properties and share your opinion with other readers!

HARLEQUIN®

A Romance FOR EVERY MOOD™

**Stay up-to-date on all your
romance-reading news with the
Harlequin Shopping Guide,
featuring bestselling authors, exciting new
miniseries, books to watch and more!**

The newest issue will be delivered right to you
with our compliments! There are 4 each year.

Signing up is easy.

EMAIL

ShoppingGuide@Harlequin.ca

WRITE TO US

HARLEQUIN BOOKS
Attention: Customer Service Department
P.O. Box 9057, Buffalo, NY 14269-9057

OR PHONE

1-800-873-8635 in the United States
1-888-343-9777 in Canada

Please allow 4-6 weeks for delivery of the first issue by mail.

THE WORLD IS BETTER WITH

Romance

Harlequin has everything from contemporary, passionate and heartwarming to suspenseful and inspirational stories.

Whatever your mood, we have a romance just for you!